How to be a Super Bitch Lawyer

By Anna Corsellis

 www.trafford.com

North America & international
toll-free: 1 888 232 4444 (USA & Canada)
phone: 250 383 6864 ◆ fax: 812 355 4082

CHAPTER ONE

Roger's gaze followed the perfect curve of the young girl's purple, satin-clad bottom that gyrated gently only inches from his open mouth. Just like two bubbles ready to burst, he thought, enjoying the view immensely. That was the precise moment, in fact, when he decided it was time for him to employ a new secretary. The old bird who had typed out the verbose letters to his worried clients was ripe for the heave-ho and a fresh face would do wonders for his morale and therefore his firm. Meade, Pullen and Co Solicitors were hanging on by the skin of their teeth as they approached the 21st century and he had to do something about it fast. Roger slipped his card into the girl's handbag and turned towards his companion, sitting in near darkness in a corner of the nightclub.

"Fancy another drink, Idris? I'm feeling rather thirsty."

Idris nodded, his face alternating between green and red with every beat of the music.

"Don't mind if I do," he gasped. "I'm rather 'ot in here."

He winced as his left thigh was crushed by the tall, chiffon clad monster of a woman who perched on his lap and was running what remained of her fingers through his blackened hair.

Roger approached the bar and, as he was just about to hand over a crisp £50 note to the barman, he happened to notice the satin-clad bottom disappearing into the Gents. 'Buggeration,' he said, making a quick exit. 'Not again.'

The next morning, Roger found himself sitting in the first class carriage of a train carrying him into London Bridge Station. His head pounded; a feeling, he thought, not very unlike a sharp nail being driven deep into his cerebral cortex. He writhed in his over-warm seat, trying desperately - but unsuccessfully - to stifle a rumbling, quinine tainted belch. Bastard gin and tonics did it every time, he thought, helping himself to another black coffee. They did make him exceedingly gassy. Particularly annoying as he was due in court that morning and he sincerely hoped that he didn't belch there. The Defendants had taken out an application to strike out his client's claim, Roger having served important documents two weeks too late, and an appearance before District Judge Smithers was, therefore, inevitable. Roger rubbed the back of his hand over his forehead and wondered what on earth he was going to say to the learned judge this time. The explanation of 'Client gone crazy, Sir. Without instructions,' had been used one time too many. His hands trembled at the thought. Two stations later Roger had decided on his plan of action. A nice, new assistant solicitor was what he needed to bail him out. Forget the secretary.

Without wasting a moment, Roger contacted the recruitment agency. A week later, Felicity Garrett, coincidentally being pert of backside and pert of brain, found herself being whisked up to Meade, Pullen and Co's

Boardroom the moment she placed an expensively heeled foot inside the office door.

'Mr Elwyn Roberts, our senior legal executive,' Roger explained. An elderly, red haired man on the opposite side of the mahogany table grinned at Felicity through uneven teeth. His orange/brown skin bulged out of his shiny, grey suit and his fingers, like exploding hot dogs, were attached to his hands by numerous gold rings. Felicity thoughtfully pulled up her long skirt to reveal two well-formed ankles. Roger immediately took a sharp intake of breath. He had indeed found the ideal candidate.

'So, Miss Garrett. Why Meade Pullen?'

'Simply because of your reputation as a fore-runner in personal injury litigation.'

Roger's eyes widened at the very thought.

'Ah, marvellous. And why did you become a solicitor?'

Happy memories of life as a law undergraduate at Cambridge, hours spent being propelled into the Cam, filled Roger's mind just as thoughts of an entirely different nature were floating behind Felicity's fragrant smile on the opposite side of the table. Quite clearly it's because I want to be a smart, highly paid professional, driving a sports car and kitted out entirely in expensive underwear by the age of thirty, Felicity almost added; visions of a high-maintenance lifestyle floating past her. That was her destiny, after all.

In reality, and this fact had been neatly brushed over in her CV, Felicity had succumbed to a brief stint at a medical school in Tooting in an attempt to placate her parents' desires for her to become a doctor. However, after failing to remove the correct organ from a laboratory rat on one occasion too many, she reluctantly agreed with the university lecturers that the medical world would be a far safer place without her. 'It's simply no good,' the Professor of Urology had bellowed at her with furrowed brow, 'to expect credit for

3

removing an obese rodent's stomach in an attempt to resolve its tendency to over-eat.'

The next day, Felicity had quickly packed her bags, waved goodbye with a manicured hand and stomped out of the hospital ward to the echo of many joyful sighs of relief from the earnest patients and staff alike.

'I've always been interested in the law,' she explained, fluttering her eyelashes at her naïve and gullible interviewer. (Indeed, having a Claim Form slapped on you whilst working for the NHS was always a realistic, and therefore interesting, possibility.) 'And joined the profession to enhance my knowledge of it whilst benefiting clients at the same time.'

Roger breathed a huge sigh of relief. He looked across at his nubile candidate. 'Miss Garrett,' he said, trying to avert his eyes from the frilly underwear peeping out from her tight shirt, 'I think I need to see you again. Could you come back for a second interview?'

FELICITY

'So, James,' Felicity barked down the telephone at her rotund boyfriend, 'the meeting went incredibly well. And they've asked me to come back for a second interview! Can you believe it?'

'Absobloominglutely, my love,' replied James in his beautifully rounded vowels, carefully cultivated by his mother, the marvellous and athletic, Mrs Peters. 'Can't wait for you to come back to the Smoke, full time.' James quietly hoped that living with Fliss might well mean more, and possibly more varied, copulation despite Felicity's insistence on a 45 minute pre coitus warning. 'I'll buy you a little pressie for doing so well,' he added, crossing his legs.

Consequently, the following week was an anxious one. His worries, momentarily quashed by visiting Peter Jones' Department Store, were only to return when he considered how to present Felicity with her new lingerie. What would her reaction be? He was well aware that his monthly night of passion was only a week away and he might be jeopardising his chances if he got her chest size wrong. Finally, though, after a number of sweaty-palmed telephone calls he arranged to meet Felicity in a Fulham wine bar on a cold, wet night.

With his drenched hands tightly gripping a plastic bag containing an enormous tent-like bra, he proposed that they live together rather than Felicity rent on her own when she returned to London.

Some 45 minutes passed until Felicity wholeheartedly agreed.

GEOFFREY

Geoffrey Carter QC stood at one of the large, sash windows in his room in Chambers overlooking Square Court. He had chosen the only room on the upper ground floor for himself as he took great pleasure in examining the facial expressions of the Temple workers carrying out their business. He had absolutely no intention whatsoever of being hidden away in the lower floor. His unshakeable view was that being a voyeur was one of the fringe benefits of being a successful Silk. It kept his finger on the pulse of Temple life and, as a result, meant that he was still a serious court player. He liked it that way.

Most activity around the Middle Temple took place just before the courts opened at ten o' clock and these were the hours that Geoffrey relished. He could think of no higher form of daylight entertainment, apart from the obvious, than examining the furrowed brows of the barristers and their clerks as they headed north to the Royal Courts of Justice on the Strand nearby. Half an hour later and Temple would be silent again. Even then, thought Geoffrey, one could still "smell" the egos and ambitions of those lawyers busily working away in Chambers on their various Briefs rippling through the quiet squares and lanes of the barristers' domains. It was an exciting place to be.

It was now past seven o' clock. The long shadows cast over his wig and gown hanging from the back of the door indicated that it was the end of his working day and, having watched the slow exodus from Square Court, he was finally alone in the quiet of his room. Geoffrey considered having a final cigarette before he set off and cautiously put his right hand on his ribcage, feeling it rise and fall before happily lighting up a Gauloise. Some life left in the old dog yet, he thought, despite the many years he had spent as a "criminal" barrister sitting in smoke-filled cells, pacifying his always-guilty clients.

As Geoffrey's career had developed, he had departed from crime and taken on more and more clinical negligence cases. These were not only much better paid than the criminal ones but also provided him with a platform from which to demonstrate his advocacy skills. Fortunately, he had built up years and years of experience, standing before Magistrates and Recorders in the criminal courts, pleading for his clients to be let off their various charges and this had put him head and shoulders above those civil litigation lawyers who had spent their years stuck in Chambers merely drafting court documents. Most of his contemporaries therefore despised him; they were jealous of this out-of town barrister who had whipped away their best clients from under their stuck-up noses. In their view, he was a criminal hack who had had a lucky break. Nothing more, nothing less.

As it turned out, Geoffrey quite agreed. He acknowledged that this fortunate turn of events had stemmed from his acquaintance with Roger Wilbraham-Evans. The two had met at a strip joint in Soho late one night and immediately hit it off having, as it transpired, a number of common interests.

Subsequently, Roger instructed Geoffrey to represent his clients who had serious, and often complex, clinical negligence claims, both deciding that it was much easier to discuss matters out of office hours in more relaxed surroundings. Geoffrey, though fully appreciating the huge opportunity that had fallen into his lap, was quite happy to work all day preparing for these cases but never, ever, at night, there being far too much entertainment to be sought. Indeed, Geoffrey found that whenever he crossed from Piccadilly to Shaftesbury Avenue, his chest tightened in anticipation of yet another informative night. He was therefore a man who had to rely solely upon his wits and the crib notes upon which he had scribbled at the last minute before trial to get him through a day in court. It should have been no surprise to him that the more studious members of the legal world continually spurned and abhorred him.

The only exception to this rule was Roger. He cared little for the views wafting around the Robing rooms in the London courts or the stuffier sets of Chambers. He concerned himself only with pleasing his wife, his clients and the occasional homosexual, in that order. Geoffrey admired him for that and was looking forward to seeing him in conference the following day.

*

Geoffrey drummed his nicotine-stained fingers on the windowsill and watched a tall, frizzy-haired girl in her mid twenties cross the square in front of him. Not a bad sight at this time of day, he thought to himself as he turned away. He pulled out his favourite brown leather chair and sat down to survey his Mont Blanc pens, earlier laid out for him by his trusty clerk, ready for action. He picked up the black ink pen, took off the lid and began writing, heading the page with the words "Counsel's Advice on Quantum" before underlining them twice. He thought for a moment and then sat back to consider the case upon which he was working. Mrs Connolly, a young mother, had died tragically following a botched hysterectomy. How could anyone allow that to happen, he asked himself? How could he ever advise as to how much the case was truly worth? A life was surely priceless.

Geoffrey walked over to the bookshelf and ran his finger along the spines of the dusty legal annuals. He lifted one out and had just started to flick through the pages when the telephone rang. It was his clerk, Archie Salt.

'Yes?' Geoffrey answered gruffly.

'Sorry to bother you, Sir,' Archie hated disturbing any of Chambers inhabitants with anything unless it involved Brief fees, 'but there's a young lady here to see you. Her name's Sarah Kelleher.'

'Bugger,' groaned Geoffrey. 'I'd forgotten she was coming. Let me have two minutes and then show her in.'

Archie looked at Sarah. He couldn't fathom what on earth Mr Carter had seen in this one. Much too large, he thought, sure that Mr Carter didn't like them when they towered above him. He always said that 'it put him off'.

'I'll take you through in a moment, Miss. Please take a seat.'

Sarah sat down on one on the sofas, picked up *The Times* newspaper and glanced at the legal appointments section at the back. Nothing interesting, she thought, apart from a part-time position in Abergavenny. Not likely. No way would she be driven out of London, she had decided, even if it meant working for the Crown Prosecution Service. God forbid!

'Mr Carter's ready for you now, Miss. Would you like to follow me?'

Sarah followed behind Archie as he marched smartly down a corridor, trying to straighten her creased skirt on every stride. She stopped abruptly behind Archie when he reached the far end and knocked twice on the large door.

'Come,' ordered a muffled voice.

Sarah was ushered into the room to be greeted by Geoffrey perching on the corner of the table, his short legs waving about in the air.

'Hello!' said Sarah. 'Very kind of you to invite me here.'

'No problem at all. My pleasure.' Geoffrey smiled through gritted teeth. He really needed to crack on with that Advice. 'Do take a seat.' He jumped down from the table and pulled out a chair for Sarah. 'I seem to recall that we met at a drinks party. Is that correct?'

'Yes. Here at the Chambers' Party, two weeks ago. I mentioned to you that I was hoping to move to another firm - I'm currently at Portshires - and you thought that you might be able to put me in touch with someone you knew.'

'Ah, yes.'

Slowly it all came back to him. Geoffrey remembered the champagne, the dreadful food and the dark dingy dungeon that was the clerks' room. At the time, Sarah had looked much prettier than the girl in front him now. Golly, he thought, his new uplifting heels really were effective; this great lump of a girl was much taller than he had earlier appreciated.

'I'm sure I must have had my dear friend, Roger Wilbraham-Evans, in mind. In fact, I'm seeing him tomorrow afternoon so I'll put in a good word. I'm sure he'll be able to sort out something for you. Let me have your 'phone number to pass on to him.' Geoffrey tore out a blank sheet of paper from his notepad and roughly pushed it along the table for Sarah to scribble down her details.

'Right then. I'm so sorry, Sally,' he said, pushing back his leather chair as he stood up. 'But I really must get on now. I do appreciate your trouble in coming in.'

Geoffrey looked at Sarah's beaming face. Far too much pan-stick, he thought. Ugh. He simply detested that feeling of lard against his skin and stood well back in case Sarah tried to kiss him.

'Now, promise you'll keep in touch,' he said, shovelling her out of the room.

Geoffrey closed the door and returned to his writing. 'Now, where was I?' He did so hate being interrupted.

Geoffrey spent the following morning in Chambers, yet again. Nowadays, he almost resented the disruption that a day in court brought. The thought that he was becoming a creature of habit, although moderately disturbing, was not sufficiently worrying for him to don his robes for a meagre case management conference. It had caused great hilarity one day in Chambers when Geoffrey had likened himself to a supermodel 'not getting out of bed for less than £10,000'. He chuckled to himself as he recalled the moment.

Geoffrey yawned, stretching his arms high above his head before pulling out the Advice that he had completed for Roger. He was quite pleased with his efforts. Although it was thorough, it left quite a bit of work for his instructing solicitor to do. After all, and although it was difficult to believe, solicitors were lawyers too and they expected to be involved in their client's cases, albeit to a limited extent. You see, he had once explained to an earnest pupil barrister, if you make the solicitor feel that they are contributing to the success of the case, they have a much stronger sense of fulfilment. A happy solicitor means return business. This Advice would give Roger enough flexibility to use his discretion during the final crunch when negotiating with the defendant's solicitors. Helpful, but not spoon-feeding, was the name of the game.

Geoffrey was about to re-read his Advice when there was a loud knock on the door and a tall, handsome man strode into the sunlit room. 'How marvellous to see you again, Roger!' Geoffrey scrambled to his feet. 'It seems like an absolute age since I saw you last. Actually,' he continued, lowering himself onto his padded chair, 'I need to discuss a separate matter with you. Nothing serious. Any chance you could drop in to *The Porkie Pie* after the conference?'

'Of course, I'd love to. Pamela's not expecting me back until late anyway.'

There was a further knock at the door and a bewildered-looking client, Mr Connolly, was shown in. The conference started chaotically and, unusually for Geoffrey, who tended to get shot of his clients well under ninety minutes, it was not until two hours thirty minutes later that day that their meeting finally ended. During that time, despite perspiring hard as he silently recalled the previous night's lap dancing "lecture" in utmost detail, Geoffrey insisted that Roger put more pressure on the Defendants to increase their current offer.

'We've been given a provisional trial date for mid July,' Roger mentioned, crossing his long fingers and looking uncommonly worried, 'and that should provide us with plenty of time to draft the Schedule of Loss.'

Roger had already decided that he would have to pass the file to someone else pretty quickly if the case was going to be dealt with at all properly, or, in fact, at all. He had important fishing dates coming up in the summer and he had no intention of missing an event. The other vital factor was that he couldn't afford to botch up another claim. It had taken him thirty years as a litigation practitioner to realise that compliance with time limits was the most important factor in civil law. If one was missed then it was time to call in the insurers; even the tiniest breach of the Court Rules always resulted in a negligence action against the firm, *goddamnit*! Mistakes were therefore extremely costly. However, Roger was fortunate in that he had been able, for various reasons, to manufacture a rather interesting secret deal with Elwyn Roberts's wealthy twin brother, Idris, which had enabled the firm to stay afloat so far without having to resort to the loss adjustors on too many occasions.

'I hope you don't mind me asking, but what on earth is a Schedule of Loss?' asked Mr Connolly. Roger writhed fretfully in his chair, hoping that the question hadn't been directed at him.

'It's the document that sets out the actual financial loss, past and future,' Geoffrey explained, having noticed Roger's disconcertion. 'You'll receive compensation for Laura's pain and suffering, in addition, but it won't be much.'

Obviously, it was hard for Mr Connolly to enjoy being part of the litigation process but at least his lawyers' grey hair and lined faces were apparent proof of sufficient experience to give him some much needed, but misplaced, confidence and he left the conference an unwisely relieved man.

Geoffrey folded up his papers and set off with Roger to walk through Temple, up past *The Devereux Pub* and then round to their favourite wine bar. Geoffrey was a regular at *The Porkie Pie* and, as always, settled himself into the booth to the right of the doorway. An obliging barman delivered a bottle of Chablis and two glasses.

Roger looked at Geoffrey. 'You know,' he said, 'there's something I've always meant to ask you.' Geoffrey looked alarmed, hoping that it wasn't going to be anything to do with his recent love of cycling home late in the nude, a hobby he'd kept under tight wraps. 'I've always wondered why you didn't become a High Court Judge. Weren't you asked?'

Geoffrey twiddled with the signet ring on his little finger. 'Why on earth would I want to do something like that? Spend my days having to listen to junior barristers fluffing their lines and fumbling over bundles of documents? No thanks!'

'I thought the prestige might appeal to you.'

'No, not me. I'm not part of the Old School. They don't want an unconventional divorced hack like me on the Bench. Anyway, the money's rotten.' Geoffrey took a tight-lipped sip from his glass. His eyes followed a young female barrister carrying a file of papers across to the bar and then balance her left buttock upon a stool.

'Actually, I need to speak to you about someone,' said Geoffrey, wishing to change the subject.

'Go on. I'm intrigued.'

'It's about a young solicitor I've met.'

'I might have guessed as much.'

'Really, she's not my type at all. Needs to lose a few pounds of flesh but possibly a good solicitor even so from what I can gather.' Geoffrey sniffed hard into his handkerchief. 'Sorry, where was I? Oh, yes. That girl,' he continued, cramming the maroon square of silk back into his trouser pocket. 'She's only got a few years' post qualification experience but seems to be quite sensible. She's currently at Portshires, I think it's called. Anyway,' he added casually, 'if you've got any space at Meade Pullen, you might like to consider her. Portshires might be going under, from what I can gather.'

'That's interesting. Golly.' Roger desperately tried to stifle a grin. 'I always thought that they did rather well out of their white collar clients. But, I guess you never can tell what's around the corner!' He paused to savour the moment, pleased to learn of another firm's poor performance. 'In fact, we might well be looking for fresh blood, er, I mean a new one. We've just interviewed a rather tasty solicitor from Southampton but Elwyn isn't convinced that she's suitable.' Roger bit his lip. 'Marvellous ankles, though,' he added, sighing heavily as he recalled the shapely bones that blossomed forth from Felicity's delicate feet. 'I guess it might be worth me meeting up with this other girl, I suppose.'

'Oh, I'm quite sure you won't want to meet her *outside* the office, if you see what I mean,' Geoffrey added hurriedly.

'Quite, quite. What did you say her name was?'

'I didn't. It's Sarah Kelleher. Look.' Geoffrey fumbled inside his jacket and handed Roger a scrap of paper. 'Here you are. I said that you would call if you were interested.'

'Great. Thanks. It might save us the cost of an agency fee and you know how tight-fisted our managing partner is. At least he would be pleased.'

'Northerner, isn't he?'

'Yes. And an exceptionally mean one at that. He's even talking about making us travel second class on trains. Can you believe it?' Roger shook his head. 'Times, they are a changing. It's not the plush lifestyle for us personal injury lawyers any more. We'll be going the same way as criminal solicitors next; south of the river.' Roger sighed heavily and polished off his glass of wine. How on earth would he manage to pay for all Pamela's hair dos, he asked himself, if there were any further cutbacks? Lank hair had always upset him, particularly over breakfast.

'Never!' Geoffrey tutted loudly, causing bewigged heads to turn and stare at the creator of such an outburst. 'Come, come now. Surely things could never get that bad?' He dabbed at his forehead with his monogrammed pocket-handkerchief. 'How about another glass to cheer you up? On me, of course, given your impecunious circumstances.'

Geoffrey was momentarily stunned into silence on learning such news from a fellow lawyer and was only able to continue speaking once champagne fizzed in flutes before them.

'Apart from the dreadful Northern invasion, how are things at Meade Pullen?'

'OK I guess. Appointing Marina as a partner was a good move. I have been reliably informed that she's got, what they call good HR skills, whatever they are.'

'Hiring Rejects, I think. But really, Roger, was it absolutely necessary to make her a partner? She isn't your stereotypical lawyer by any stretch of the imagination.' A shiver ran down Geoffrey's spine. A few years ago, following one of Chambers' party, Marina had cornered him in a broom cupboard and the incident had left him unable to look at floor polish without trembling.

'You see, Geoffrey,' Roger continued, 'we had a problem in that our Union client was just a bit, shall we say, *right on*. The General Secretary - you know, Elwyn Roberts's brother, Idris - told me that he found it odd, in our day and age, that we only had male partners. Marina was the only person who faintly matched the female gender.'

'Are you sure?'

'Yes, we only had male lawyers.'

'No, no. I mean are you sure that Marina is female? Remember that I've been in close proximity to her.' The detergent smells stifling the air in the dark claustrophobic broom cupboard filled his mind. 'And I'm not at all sure myself,' he whispered. Geoffrey looked agitated, his eyes twitching quickly from left to right. 'You know, those doctors can work magic *down below*.'

Roger considered Geoffrey's remark. 'Maybe you're right. She does, actually, remind me of Madame Taloolah at Julian's Panther Palace,' he chortled. 'Perhaps we could go there later to see if Marina is moonlighting?'

Geoffrey nodded his head slowly in approval.

'I think that's an excellent idea, my friend. I'll get the young lad to call us a cab.'

MARINA

During the evening before her second interview at Meade Pullen and Co, Felicity lay in the bath at their flat surrounded by vanilla scented aromatherapy candles, warbling in a shrill, querulous voice as she tried to envisage the partner whom she would be meeting; Marina Johansson. She must be Danish with such an exotic name, she thought. Definitely blonde. Probably quite tall and slim.

Felicity's skin had begun to shrivel up in the hot, foam-filled water when her mobile, perched perilously on the edge of the bath, rang. She pushed her flowery bath cap up over her ear and bellowed at her frustrated housemate, desperate to brush her teeth, to stop hammering on the door.

'Hi, Fliss,' said the round voweled voice at the end of the telephone. 'It's James. How are you, my love?'

'Fine. But be quick.'

'Sorry. I won't keep you. I just wanted to let you know about the travel arrangements to the hotel tomorrow. I've managed to borrow my parents' Land Cruiser so we can all cram in together.'

'What, even Lydia?'

'Yes. There's just enough room. And Mark.'

'What about his silly wife? What's her name? I can never remember.'

'Rebecca. She can't make it so Mark will be on his own.'

Felicity pulled out the plug, rolling her eyeballs at the damp-blotched ceiling as she considered the prospect of a weekend away. A number of months ago, she had organised a short holiday with their friends at the Copse House Hotel. Unfortunately, Lydia, James' flat mate, had included herself in the party and, rather annoyingly for Felicity, had recently tried passing herself off as a non-practising lesbian in the hope that it might generate some erotic interest. There had been no success, thus far, and Felicity felt that it would spoil the weekend if Lydia tried to make a pass at any one of the girls or, more importantly, herself.

With the telephone dangling from her hand, she mulled over her worsening relationship with Lydia. Initially, there had been little animosity between the two girls. However, as Felicity spent more and more of her weekends at the shared flat, Lydia, worried that she would have to move out, began to perform increasingly tiresome acts. Only a week earlier, Felicity had had to purchase a new toothbrush after strongly suspecting that her current one had been used to groom Lydia's pet hamster. There had, of course, been a sullen denial from Lydia who, James pointed out in support of her defence, made concerted efforts never to brush her own hair let alone freshen up a rodent.

'So come round to the flat as soon as you've finished the interview,' James continued, oblivious to Felicity's momentary diversion from their conversation. 'I'm really looking forward to going away, aren't you? The hotel sounds fantastic.'

Felicity hesitated for a moment before replying, seeing splinters appear around the bathroom's doorknob. 'Yes. I guess so. Actually James, I'm really tired and I've got to get up early to catch the train at six tomorrow morning, so I'll go now.'

'OK. Right. I love you.'

Felicity put down the phone. She did love James but had tired of his predictability sometimes. Thinking back, she really had found him more exciting and sometimes even vaguely attractive when he was up to his lap dancing antics. Now there was only Lydia left to bicker over.

Felicity dried herself as she considered the situation. There was no alternative. She would have to think of a way to spice up their relationship; the only other option was to end it. Maybe she should have tried the pole dancing lessons at his mother's church as Mrs Peters had suggested? It might make a change from yoga and her inner thighs could do with a bit of firming up. Felicity recalled that Mrs Peters had been attending the classes for a few months now and had recently eagerly demonstrated her abilities to the amazement of the parish members by clamping the vicar against a pew for a few minutes longer than could be called decent. He had been so traumatised by the event that the Easter Bonnet parade had had to be called off. Obviously, James' mother had not been too popular after the incident, but did she care? Heck, she did not! She had said that she had other fish to fry and had stomped off, giving the churchwarden a swift kick in the shins as she left.

Early the following morning, Felicity arrived at King's Cross Station and, within a few minutes, had reached Meade Pullen's offices. She knocked on the rickety door and peered through its dirt-ridden glass to see a kilt-wearing receptionist jabbing suspiciously at a few buttons like an incompetent fencer faced with an angry cobra. Felicity opened the door and approached the man sitting behind a miniscule desk.

'Helloo?' he said, mumbling croakily into the phone. 'There's a lassy here fur yer, Miss Johansson. Her nem? Hang oan.' The receptionist placed his hand over the mouthpiece and looked earnestly at Felicity.

'Felicity Garrett.'

'She's callin' hersel' Felicity Garrett.'

Having barked in his mysterious accent at his employer, the Receptionist tremulously replaced the evil telephone receiver, all the time eyeing Felicity warily as if she were from another planet.

'She'll be doon in a manute or so and asked if yee'd like te tek a seat.'

Felicity had only a few moments to wait before a delicate voice rang out through the cold winter air.

'Miss Garrett?'

Felicity rose to her feet. She turned slowly and nearly screamed. The sight before her was quite shocking. Where was the slim blonde she had anticipated? Instead of a glamorous, leggy beauty here was a short, white-faced, ginger-haired woman whose body mass index was surely in excess of 45.

'Yes?' Felicity stared in amazement.

'Hi. I'm Marina Johansson.'

'*Really*?!' Felicity momentarily lost her balance as she staggered around Reception on her unsuitable heels.

'Thanks for coming in again.' Marina shook Felicity's hand tenderly in her own scarily small one. 'Would you like to follow me?'

When they finally reached Miss Johansson's room, the larger of the two solicitors sat down cautiously behind her desk leaving Felicity to drag a wooden chair across the stained, grey carpet. For once in her life, she was dumbfounded by the situation. She had prepared herself mentally for a bit of a challenging morning being grilled by a successful, city-type lawyer. Yet here she was in front of someone who looked as if she might be more suited to a life in the circus.

'I gather that your meeting with Mr Wilbraham-Evans went well,' Marina said politely, tucking her ankles tattooed with red dragons beneath her warping seat.

'Yes, I thought so.' A few ginger hairs protruding from Marina's chin shimmered gently in the cool air and distracted Felicity momentarily. 'He was very charming.'

'Whatever,' continued Marina waving her hand around her desk, 'before we go any further, I'd like to give you a little information about the firm. If you did join us I would want you to be fully aware of what you'd be taking on. Essentially, apart from being a fabulous lawyer, you would be expected to attend the nights out that we have with our Union client.' Marina paused to laugh unrestrainedly at a private joke. 'You see,' she said, once her thighs had stopped reverberating against each other in glee, 'we only have one main client, The Camping Creators Union, and, as such, we have to ensure that we keep them as happy as possible. Fortunately, they appreciate our provision of good beer more than good legal results so we've managed to keep them happy for a number of years now. But, if we lost their retainer, well…' Marina looked about her dingy room, unaware that it could be anything but a pleasant place to spend one's working life. 'You can imagine what would happen to this place.' Felicity's eyes widened. 'So,' Marina continued, 'now that I've scared you, 'I can tell you not to worry as the General Secretary of the Union is an old friend of one of the partners here. Now,' she said, sitting back in her dangerously creaking chair, 'is there anything I've mentioned today that you would like me to expand upon?'

Felicity shifted uncomfortably in her chair; Marina's "fairy" voice was starting to scare her. She couldn't think straight. Her palms became clammy. Marina's vast, sweaty bosoms were obliterating her line of vision and all she knew was that she wanted to get out of that room, and fast, so she replied quickly by saying that Marina and Roger had pretty much covered everything, thank you very much.

Marina guided Felicity out into the fog filling Gray's Inn Road and heaved herself back up to her office. She dialled Roger's extension number as soon as she was able to speak.

'Hi Roger. It's Marina.'

'Oh, hello,' Roger replied, rubbing his weary eyes.

'I've just interviewed Felicity Garrett. She seems very capable, I accept, but I'm not so sure about her getting on with the clients. I think she's a bit prissy, don't you?'

'Oh, I'm sure she'll be fine. They probably thought the same thing about me when I started here!'

Marina paused for a few seconds to avoid having to comment. 'I suggest we wait until we see the other applicants before taking a final decision,' she replied curtly.

'Maybe, but I actually rather liked her. She's a bit different from our usual intake.' Roger could hear Marina groan softly on the other end of the phone. 'Anyway, I'll leave it for you to deal with,' he added, these being his favourite words and not wishing to upset the only female partner in the firm.

'Another matter which I need to raise with you is the appointment of Elwyn's sister-in-law as a replacement for Janet Parks, the practice manager.' Marina ceased moaning, now safe in the knowledge that Roger was once again compliant and not having any original thought.

'I did hear through the Meade Pullen grapevine that Janet was thinking of leaving.'

'Yes, sadly. I gather it followed a rather difficult conversation she had with Elwyn. Something about a regular provision of pastries for the staff. There was a mention of carrot cake in particular and all I can gather is that Janet felt she was simply not up to the task.'

'Sounds like a tricky one.'

'Indeed. Although at least Elwyn has been able to get his sister-in-law on board without any difficulty.'

'But, you know, I'm never quite sure about that side of the family. Where does all that money come from? It doesn't add up to me. Surely manufacturing camping equipment can't make that much money?'

'Who knows?' Marina held her breath, wondering if Roger had ever caught sight of the dragon tattoos on her ankles. Was her secret safe? Had Roger ever guessed that she was, in fact, Elwyn's little sister?

'And I guess it must be useful for Elwyn too, having all those handouts from his relatives. You know, that's how he funds his gold ring collection.'

'Really?' replied Marina, comforted by Roger's seemingly innocent remarks.

'You don't think that Elwyn's twin has anything to do with Janet's departure, do you?'

'I have no hesitation in saying that it is most certainly so. Elwyn couldn't survive without his carrot cake and in particular one that originates from his sister-in-law's six fingered hands.'

'But why would she want to work for us? Surely her husband has got more than enough cash to last them a lifetime?'

'Apparently she's decided to make use of her secretarial skills. She feels she needs a bit of independence away from the camping empire. And I guess she's worried about taking up any more hobbies, given what's happened to her fingers, or lack of, anyway.'

'You're probably right. Let's hope she doesn't lose any more digits or we might have a crisis of our own.'

'Indeed.'

As Felicity made her way to Putney Bridge, she thought about the interview and what to make of Marina Johanssen. How had someone like her become a partner by the age of, what, she guessed, 35? Was it that she had slept with one of the partners? Most unlikely. Any explicit visions of Marina in bed made her inclined to vomit wildly. Had she blackmailed one of the partners after finding out some secret information? This was possible, but, again, unlikely although she did seem a trifle odd. Alternatively, did the other partners need a female on board for some peculiar reason? This was the most likely answer. After all, they would have to be politically correct if they were striving to gain an Investors In People Award and the main benefit from that was obvious: a reduction in their Liability Insurance. On the other hand, could she just be a good lawyer? Was that all that was really necessary? Surely not?

What Felicity didn't realise was that her own future, just as Marina's, lay in the hands of an orange/brown-faced man who sat high on a Cotswolds hillside.

A PLEASANT WEEKEND AWAY

The Copse House Hotel was set deep in the heart of the rolling Cotswolds countryside and had been described in the beaten up 1995 Hotel Guide as being "recently refurbished in 1980's design chic with quality dining in Ye Olde Candlelight Restaurant". James and Felicity, having spent two long hours veering across the motorway lanes encountering numerous 'bloody awful' drivers, finally reached their destination and were quickly shown into *The Merkin* bedroom. Felicity's eyes immediately fell upon the expensive toiletries on display. The good thing about being the party organiser, she felt, however tiresome it might be, was that you could always choose the best room for yourself. Felicity undid the cap on a small bottle containing the hotel's lavender body cream and squeezed a blob onto her cold hands, massaging it gently into her skin. With her fingers softened to perfection, she removed her boots and lay on the large bed to practise her pilates breathing techniques.

As Felicity worked out, James staggered into the bedroom carrying her heavy bags of luggage. He fell onto the bed and gazed longingly at his girlfriend. 'Tasty,' he muttered as something stirred predictably within. He watched her chest rise and fall and, unable to resist Felicity lying in a horizontal position, lunged at her clumsily. 'Is there any way that we could possibly forego the forty five minute warning?' he begged, rather crudely, thought Felicity, who was somewhat taken aback by her boyfriend's ill-timed actions.

'I really don't think so, James,' she replied squirming across the bed out of arm's reach. 'My breathing will be put all out of sync.'

'Please?' James gasped desperately as if his loins were being crushed. 'We are on holiday after all.'

'Oh, all right then.' Felicity flicked her hair up into a ponytail so that James wouldn't tweak it with his elbow at an inopportune moment. 'But only if you're sure you can't wait until after supper.'

James shook his head.

'And no flagellation,' she added. 'I haven't the patience and my wrist is still aching since the last time.'

Slowly, as Felicity undid her frilly bra, she visibly brightened, recalling her grandmother's wise words. Their unanticipated romp would be 'as good as money in the bank'.

'But don't assume that there'll be a repeat performance later on,' she growled, throwing her tiny feet into the air.

*

At breakfast the next morning, their original plans to visit Cheltenham nearby were changed. Felicity had wisely used the time spent lying on her back "entertaining" James by reading the hotel's blurb about the area and suggested that they should visit the nearby arboretum instead. After all, she had told them, it was only a few miles away and they could probably make it there in about forty minutes if they borrowed the hotel's bicycles.

James rolled his eyes. As far as he was concerned, London was inhabited by only two sorts of people; those who walked to the Tube station and those who took taxis and he was most certainly one of the latter.

'I could meet you there by car, if you like,' he suggested, rather optimistically. 'Actually, Fliss, I think my right knee might be playing up. It might be a good idea if I stayed here.' James grabbed his leg and winced dramatically.

Felicity tensed. 'Phooey, James! It will do you good to get a bit of exercise. You know as well as I do that you need to shift some lard and now's a good time to start.'

James picked at his scrambled egg, looking bleak.

'Look, darling, you need to face facts,' Felicity persisted. 'You've got a fat middle-aged woman's arse and if you don't do something about it I might seriously put your name down for more line-dancing lessons.'

James squeezed another dollop of ketchup onto his plate and looked over at Felicity, memories of his cowboy-hatted nightmare flooding back.

'If you must know,' he replied, buoyed up with machismo as he always was in the 24-hour period following sex, 'I've spoken to Mummy about my expanding belly and I've already started a new diet, the details of which shall unfold over the weekend. Now, if you don't mind, I'll finish off my well-earned breakfast.'

Stunned by James' defiance, Felicity glared at the slabs of bacon that lay on his plate and thought back to her days at medical school, avidly recalling the words of wisdom that fell from the authoritative lips of the Professor of Colorectal Surgery. 'There's nothing as rewarding as a good bowel movement,' he had said after performing a particularly gruesome and messy ileostomy.

Felicity zealously devoured her bowl of bran.

Lydia, meanwhile, was busy smoking a cigarette and flicking ash onto the remains of her ravaged sausages. 'So, Lyd.' Felicity coughed. 'James and I have decided to give you a little treat.' Lydia blew out a smoke ring and watched it crawl across the breakfast table. 'Oh, yeah?'

Felicity fanned the smoke away and continued. 'We've booked you in for a day's treatment at the hotel spa. Top-to-toe cleansing and makeover including a bikini wax.' Lydia looked terrified. 'They just whip 'em out. You won't have to worry about depilation for weeks.' Here at this discreet Cotswold hotel, Felicity was finally able to wreak some revenge on Lydia for filling James' flat with rodents.

Lydia had not prepared her nether regions for close scrutiny for many years and the initial thought of some stranger fiddling about there filled her with horror. Or did it? This could be the start of something, or even someone, new. More pertinently, she had recently been introduced to a rather short, elderly gentleman bedecked in a fine set of plastic teeth who, astonishingly, had taken a shine to her, particularly enjoying her tales of Felicity's trumpeting Dutch cap that kept her awake at night. A slow smile spread over her face. 'Great!' she said. 'Where do I go?'

'Just down to the salon. And make sure they sort out your nostrils as well,' Felicity barked before hopping onto her bicycle.

Only a few hours later, Lydia had not only become the proud owner of two hairless legs, no longer fetlocked, but also of two peculiarly large 'breasts' that pointed unnaturally towards the Heavens, semi-encased in a tight, sequinned top. Even her eyelashes had been heavily encrusted with glitter.

Later that evening, when everyone was dressed for dinner and seated in the hotel restaurant, Felicity explained the gist of the private conversation she had earlier had with James. The party of friends listened in awe.

'Don't get too close to James,' she called out. 'He's on the "egg" diet! All light and fluffy on the inside.'

'It's actually quite technical,' muttered James, turning red with embarrassment. He was astounded that his so-called girlfriend could divulge such confidential information, even having the brazen audacity to guffaw loudly when he had shown her the yellow post-it notes stuck to the inside of his navy blue blazer by his mother as a constant reminder of his goals. 'Anyway, I think it's working,' he added, tucking his pink paper napkin into his collar. 'I've lost a few pounds since I started.'

James was about to launch into a great explanation of the intricacies of egg dieting when a lithe, olive-skinned waiter interrupted him. 'Just to let you know that the Baron sends his compliments and says that you should not hesitate to let him know if there is anything you desire to make your evening more enjoyable.'

'Well, a bottle of whisky should do the trick,' said Mark as he looked around the dimly lit room.

In the corner of the restaurant sat a brown leathery-faced man looking not too dissimilar in appearance to Englebert Humperdinck. He waved at Mark and then hobbled over to their table with the aid of two gold encrusted crutches.

'Let me introduce myself,' he said bowing low and leering at his open-mouthed audience. '*I* am Baron Von Roberts the Fifth. And I am pleased to meet you all.'

'Likewise, I'm sure,' replied James, grudgingly putting down his menu having just spotted the words "double cheese soufflé".

'Now, boys and girls. I am sure I could provide some pleasure for you this fine evening. I have a number of exciting celebrity friends staying with me at my humble abode and you young people look as if you might enjoy their company. Please come with me and be my honoured guests.'

During this speech and, despite his disabilities, the Baron's head had gradually become immersed in Felicity's small decolletage, much to her astonishment and, moreover, inconvenience. She pushed his oily, blackened head away. 'We'll think about it, thanks, Baron. We haven't eaten yet.'

'Not a problem, my dear. My cook will prepare whatever your heart desires. Even oysters,' tempted the Baron, clicking his fingers rapidly as if preparing the molluscs himself.

'The thing is,' said James, 'I've brought a strawberry meringue pie specially prepared by my mother.' He spoke very slowly as if the Baron was hard of hearing and very old despite his youthful looks, however created. 'And I was rather looking forward to eating it. It's in the hotel kitchen now. It was supposed to be a surprise for everyone.'

Felicity looked at James in horror. 'Please tell me you're joking,' she begged, shaking her head. 'This egg thing is going a bit too far, don't you think? Anyway, I'm not eating anything that's been in your mother's fridge. Your dear father licks each and every item first before he stashes it away. Everything, just everything, gets covered with his spittle. Why does he always do that, darling?'

'I guess it was something he was trained to do when he was in the SAS.'

'Friends, friends!' exclaimed the Baron, 'now is not the time for discussing hygiene. It is time for making new acquaintances and sharing the night. Come, before I change my mind.' The Baron took another step back, aware that Lydia was peering at the orange/brown tidemark skirting his jaw-line. 'Two of my companions this evening are Formula

Three racing car drivers and they will escort you to my home. Let us depart. You can tell me your names on the way.'

So, that was settled. They all stood up and followed the Baron out of the restaurant and into the starry night, not knowing what the adventure might bring.

Outside the hotel, the Baron arranged for his guests to be driven home in a variety of personalised number plated cars. As *Baron 1* glided to a standstill before the hotel door, a black-capped chauffeur jumped out and deftly opened the car door for the Baron and Felicity to climb in.

'Straight home please, Dominic,' the Baron roared at his driver before turning awkwardly round to Felicity. 'Dominic is not only my chauffeur but also my butler,' he explained politely, his injured knee dangling over his crutch. 'He's what they call *multi-talented*. But, he *is* Scottish so you may not understand every word he says. I'll translate for you if necessary.'

The limousine sped off into the night and, after turning right out of the hotel's gates, they continued on down the winding country lanes. All the while Felicity had to flatten herself against the windows as far away as possible from the Baron's wandering hands. He had no alternative, he explained, but to sit close to her with his legs wide apart because of his ankle injuries. 'I was this far away from an amputation,' he explained holding his forefinger and thumb an inch apart and lightly brushing against Felicity's small breasts as he did so.

Felicity looked closely at the Baron's hands as he tinkered with her sequins. Those fingers were like exploding hot dogs, she thought. Where had she seen fingers like that before? She racked her brain, trying to remember.

'Look! Here we are!'

The Baron sat bolt upright as the car turned left through electronic gates smothered with gold paint and into an elm tree-lined driveway. Felicity could see the lights of a house in the distance and, as they drew closer, a mock Tudor mansion materialised. 'What a beautiful place!' Felicity exclaimed, her eyes lighting up.

'Thank you,' said the Baron. 'I bought it along with the title as a Valentine gift for my wife. Our love life has improved no end since she's been able to call herself The Baroness.'

'I'm not surprised!' replied Felicity, secretly sneering at such lower middle class extravagance. Oh, how the nouveau live! 'And how exactly did you make your fortune?' she teased. 'Or was it inherited?'

'I was wondering when you might ask me that question,' the Baron replied, leaning back against the soft, black leather seat. 'You see, I am an *inventor*!' he explained. 'I developed the first edible tent; it's called the Club Scout. Essentially, all I did was create a tent that, instead of folding it up after use, you simply eat it. In my youth I recall that the worst bit about camping was putting your kit away.'

'But what's it made of?'

The Baron beamed in delight, his whitened teeth glowing like the eponymous worm. 'Now, that's the secret! But, I am at liberty to tell you that the camping poles are in fact over blown sausages that slot one into the other until you've made the appropriate length of pole for your canvas. After you've finished, you can simply fry them up. Easy as pie!'

Felicity gasped appreciatively. 'What a marvellous invention!'

'Why thank you. I think so, too.' The Baron shifted forwards in his seat as the car came to a halt. 'And here we are!' he exclaimed.

He led the way up to a heavy, oak front door, removed the large key that had been dangling round his neck on a chain and inserted it into the bronze keyhole. 'Oh dear,' he said, fiddling desperately with the lock. 'I think my wife must have bolted the door. I do hope she hasn't retired to bed. She hates being disturbed from her, er, sleep.'

Felicity was horrified. Surely the Baroness would not take too kindly to having her home swamped by strangers?

'Are you certain that it's alright for me to be here?' she asked, desperately hoping that her presence would not be the cause of any matrimonial disharmony.

'Of course it's no problem,' the Baron replied, demonstrating misplaced bravado. 'We've got all those other guests with us anyway so a few more won't make any difference.'

At that moment, a tall, statuesque, woman dressed in a long green chiffon gown wrenched open the door. Her eyes narrowed as hate shot out of them at her husband; his new, attractive young companion distinctly displeased her.

'Sorry to bother you, darling,' the Baron grovelled, hovering nervously on his crutches in the dark porch. 'I've brought some friends home with me. I hope you don't mind,' he added, cowering like a beaten dog as her great form blocked out the light flowing from his palatial home. 'I've been telling them what a wonderful wife you are.'

'Really?'

His wife swooped away into the hallway like a demonic mermaid, the green shimmer of floating material cascading behind her. 'I was on the verge of intromission when you disturbed me,' she bawled into the darkness. 'I'm going back upstairs.'

'What was that she said?' asked the Baron. 'Something about adverts on the telly?' Felicity raised her eyebrows. She followed her host into the enormous hallway panelled with dark wood. Suits of armour were squeezed into each corner and Baronial portraits hung from every wall. A solitary chaise longue had been placed in front of a roaring fire and next to its hearth lay a tiger-skin rug.

The butler, now wearing a kilt, loomed out of the shadows. 'Pink champagne, please, Dominic,' the Baron ordered, 'and some canapes as well. We don't want our guests getting too tipsy, do we? They might end up doing something they regret!'

Whilst Felicity supped champagne, she heard a great deal of commotion as her companions arrived. It turned out that the racing car drivers had had a mock race en route which had left their passengers quite shaken, wide-eyed and with their hair standing on end. Lydia was now the proud owner of only one of her "breasts", the other having escaped out of an open car window on a particularly sharp bend in the road. With hands-a-tremble, they gratefully accepted the cigars being handed round by Dominic and stood in the grand hallway admiring the Baron's possessions.

As the men stood puffing contentedly on tobacco filled torpedoes, the Baron offered to show them round his home.

'We could start down here and work our way up to the bedrooms,' he suggested, staring imploringly at his guests and fiddling anxiously with his blackened hair. Felicity stared hard at the floor, not wishing to catch her host's gaze and, only after an embarrassingly long silence, James and Mark volunteered to take up the Baron's generous offer. The Baron clapped his hands excitedly and whipped round before making his way towards the grand staircase with James and Mark following meekly behind 'oohing' and 'aahing' appreciatively at the fine antiques, most still bearing their price tags. Eventually, they reached the mansion's upper floors where, after countless bedroom doors had been flung open to reveal numerous dishevelled guests, they finally came upon an empty one. Once inside, the Baron unlocked a French Armoire and hauled out a pair of Napoleonic breeches and jacket.

'Here, try these on,' he said, thrusting the garments at James.

James held the items at arms' length, feeling the Baron's eyes burning into his back and elsewhere and hoped desperately that they would be too small for him. Moreover, he remembered that he was wearing an old pair of "Wallace and Gromit" underpants that had been a gift from his mother some five years ago and which had become worn in inconvenient places.

The Baron grew impatient. 'Just give them a go,' he urged. 'If they fit, you can keep them. They're worth a pretty penny.'

James slowly peeled off his outer clothes and, using Mark to shield himself from the Baron's gaze, squeezed himself into the tight breeches. His fingers fiddled clumsily with the gold plated buttons and he had only managed to secure two when the bedroom door swung open. In stepped the Baroness, enjoying a post-coital cigarette. She blew smoke out through her nose like a dragon in delight as she spied yet another potential victim. 'Mmm,' she murmured, dangerously. 'Something for the weekend?' She closed the door and leaned her tall frame against it. There was no escape. Even the Baron grew anxious.

'Well, hello?' she continued, licking her lips and twisting her six fingers (two fingers, one thumb on each hand) around her black, waist length hair. 'And what have we here?'

Without wasting a moment, the Baroness marched over to James and, gripping him with her talons, led him away to her lair. There really was nothing he could do apart from quiver and jabber incoherently. 'I may be some time,' he quipped, trying to make light of the situation.

Mark, though momentarily struck dumb by the Baron's underwater monster of a wife, made chase as soon as he could politely leave the room without offending his host. He re-opened one door after the other but James was nowhere to be seen. Finally, having given up hope of tracing his friend, Mark returned to the grand hallway where he found Felicity and Lydia still roasting cosily in front of the fire with some of the racing car drivers.

'Come on,' he said looking directly at Felicity, hoping that he had correctly interpreted her flirtatious comments about taut buttocks at dinner. 'Who wants to go exploring with me?'

Lydia, meanwhile, had made inroads with one of the Formula Three drivers despite the disappearance of one of her "breasts" and was hoping that an intimate event might occur at any moment. 'Not me, thanks,' she replied. 'I have plans of my own.'

'I will,' exclaimed Felicity. She placed her champagne flute on the sideboard next to a stuffed fox and followed Mark down one of the unlit corridors. They peeped into each and every room, reeling in awe at the Baron's opulent knick-knacks, until they finally reached a door half way down the hallway that, once opened, revealed a beautifully extravagant music room. At one end, so the notice above the instrument informed them, was Elgar's pianola and, on seeing it, Felicity marched straight over before carefully opening its lid.

'Do you think it would be OK if I had a go?' she whispered, running her dainty hands over the ivory keys.

Felicity sat on the stool, carefully straightening out her long sequined dress behind her and belted out *Fur Elise* like a honky-tonk player in a pub. She was note perfect; the thousands of pounds worth of music lessons clearly having been well spent.

'Marvellous, Fliss! I had no idea you were so talented!' Mark breathed into her left ear as he straddled the piano stool next to her. He hummed along with the tune, encouraging Felicity to play on. What a kind man, thought Felicity, astutely aware that her keyboard skills were far from tolerable.

Mark was indeed a kind man but this trait, in its heightened form, tended to reveal itself in a very tactile mode. Sometimes, he just could not stop himself and, on this occasion, unable to resist the rise and fall of Felicity's neat chest, he placed his hand on her left breast and massaged it gently, hoping that she wouldn't notice, being caught up in the music, and so on. In fact, Felicity found, much to her own distaste, that she was indeed enjoying herself so much that she inadvertently added numerous arpeggios to the tune and only removed Mark's loitering hand after the very last trill had trickled through the winter air.

'Did you enjoy that?' she asked modestly.

'Quite so but I always thought it was shorter.'

Mark raised one bushy eyebrow. Quick as a flash, he lunged forward, pressing his mouth hard against her mouth with full throttle, gripping her thin arms tightly. Initially, Felicity found this direct approach marginally unpleasant being used, by now, to James' more slobbery embrace and she experienced a real urge to retch as the tip of Mark's tongue stretched almost successfully for her epiglottis.

They rolled about the room snorting and gyrating, dragging at each other's clothes. Mark, crazed with delight, tore at Felicity's lacy brassiere until a pert nipple broke free from its under-wired cage. Felicity, as ever, responded appropriately. 'My,' she gasped, catching a glimpse of his bulging trousers. 'What a mighty organ!'

Mark was, by now, wild with lust. Such dirty talk had nigh on polished him off and sweat poured down his forehead. He trembled violently at the thought of pleasuring Felicity, his fingers fumbling with her flowery pants as his own member fought its way through the hole in his y-fronts, stabbing Felicity with a vengeance. Sadly, no longer able to contain himself, his "delight" released itself all over her ball-gown and beyond.

'Good grief,' grimaced Felicity. 'It's just like Superglue.'

Who knows how long the pair would have rolled around on the parquet floor had they not been disturbed by Dominic? The butler entered the room in a rage. Admittedly, he was quite content to change soiled sheets but scrubbing permeated wood was another matter. He yelled in an incoherent accent at the courting couple who, unable to decipher his words, surmised by virtue of his facial expressions that their presence was most certainly not desired. Felicity, horribly humiliated at being caught with her silver dress and satin bow around her ears, hastily scrambled to her feet and left the room with Mark close behind.

As they walked back to join the others there was something else that was bothering Felicity, something about Dominic, the butler/driver. He, too, looked familiar. Was it the way he had dabbed at the parquet floor, just like an incompetent fencer faced with a cobra? What *was* it about this place? She couldn't put her finger on it and it was *very* irksome.

Felicity sloped along the dark corridor deep in thought until she reached the great hallway. She found Lydia and the driver cuddled up close to each other in front of the fire.

'Where's James?' she asked.

'I think the Baroness offered to show him the wine cellar so I assume he's doing a bit of tasting. Anyway, I'm sure he'll be back soon.' Lydia removed the racing car driver's loitering hand from her knee. 'The Baron's asked us if we'd like to join him in a spot of tennis here tomorrow morning,' she said, winking at the driver. 'Apparently, he likes to play early, about 8am, and he's suggested that we stay here tonight to ensure an early start. Clearly, there are plenty of bedrooms.'

Felicity, who had retrieved her champagne flute, spewed forth wine like trapped water from a hose. 'You've got to be joking!' she gasped, horrified at the proposal. She glared at Lydia harshly, drying her face with the back of her hand. 'I think we should all make a hasty exit right now, whilst we've got the chance.'

Lydia sat up. She had spent the evening nuzzling the driver's ear and planning what she would do to him, particularly now that she had rid herself of about three kilograms of body hair. What was being offered was a slice of intimacy and she could use some practice before she could confidently grapple with the old man back in London.

'But we can't get back to the hotel now!' she cried out desperately. 'The racing drivers have drunk far too much booze to drive!'

Throughout the evening Lydia had become almost demented with lust. She had systematically plied the driver sitting next to her with sufficient alcohol to ensure a one hundred percent success rate, having already forgiven him for taking the bend too quickly thereby resulting in the loss of one of her bosoms.

'And that weird chauffeur or butler or whatever he is, disappeared down the corridor ten minutes ago with some floor polish in his hand looking pretty fed up. We daren't ask him to take us back now.' A slow smile spread across Lydia's face as she felt her lower regions become fired up. 'Anyway,' she added, 'I'm not even sure that he could understand what we were saying. He sounded to me as if he came from Timbuktoo.'

Mark and Felicity sat in silence, polishing off Dominic's strange delicacies (were they varieties of black pudding, Felicity wondered? There was something distinctly carnal about them). They both knew what lay ahead for them if they remained; certainly it would not involve getting much beauty sleep and each shivered in turn at the thought of the Baron and/or his demonic wife salivating over them.

They sat in the great hall for some time, gripping their empty glasses until a side door opened and the Baroness glided out in bare feet like an ice skating queen flushed with victory. She came to a halt beside the fireplace just before James appeared, moments later, striding out with a suspicious spring in his step.

Felicity stood up. 'We're thinking about leaving now,' she said curtly, smiling through pinched lips at the unruffled James.

'Oh really?' he replied coolly, surprising Felicity with his extraordinary lack of compliance. Surely, by now, he was outside the 24 hour-bravado-after-sex-period, she thought? He should be like a little lamb, all complacent and woolly. Felicity smelt a rat.

James bravely ignored Felicity's glare. 'Do we really have to?" he continued. 'We've got loads of cigars here, booze, whatever!' He took a sneaky peek sideways at the Baroness. 'And just look at the place!' James waved his arms at the medieval artefacts adorning the room to add weight to his plea.

The Baroness stepped forward. 'I'll drive,' she said. 'I haven't been drinking so I'll take those of you who want to go.' She picked out the car keys from a silver cigar box and twirled them around the two fingers of her right hand. 'My advice is to go back to the hotel.' Her hawk-eyes narrowed suddenly. 'You'll be far more comfortable there.'

The Baroness had not been impressed with James' feeble attempts at foreplay in the cellar; she liked a bit of a challenge and her new plaything hadn't turned out to be anywhere near as feisty as she had hoped. The "Wallace and Gromit" underpants had completely sealed James' fate and a swift expulsion out of her home was the only acceptable option as far as she was concerned. 'James,' she hissed, glancing at the withering male before her. 'I insist that you, being the largest, sit in the front.'

The party trouped towards the large 4x4 wheel drive vehicle and hopped in. Lydia stayed behind, hoping that her waxing session might finally be appreciated. Screeching around the countryside lanes, the Baroness swiftly reached the hotel. She braked sharply, skidding across the gravel and ultimately came to a stomach-churning halt. The occupants of the car lurched forward and fell out of the car onto the driveway. They watched as the Baroness sped off into the night, the tail of her chiffon gown, having been caught in the car door, fiercely whipping the tarmac road as she propelled her vehicle around tight corners.

*

Five hours later, Felicity awoke and beadily surveyed James stretched out on his back next to her, at peace with the world and snoring heavily. She thought back to the episode with the Baroness. Quite clearly James had been up to no good, revealing his libido in such a carefree manner to a practical stranger but, on the other hand, it made her feel slightly less guilty about the incident with Mark in the music room. Felicity looked at James once more, transfixed by a rivulet of saliva trickling out of the corner of his mouth. Did she love him, she asked herself? Perhaps. Whatever. Either way, although he was an annoying slob, she'd be damned if any smart arsed, six-fingered temptress, or anyone else for that matter tried to turn his head. There was no alternative, she decided, but for her to move in with him in London. All she had to do was to ensure that she was offered a position at Meade Pullen and she reckoned she had just discovered a way to achieve that. She shoved James hard.

'James. You're snoring and when you're not doing that, you're grinding your teeth. I can't possibly sleep.'

James woke with a start. 'What? What?' he said, moaning loudly and turning over. The elastic in his underpants was cutting into his skin but he was too hungover to care.

'Wake up. You're making too much noise. I can't bear it!'

Felicity flung back the duvet and hung her feet out over the sides of the bed. Inch by inch, she managed to drag herself across the room and finally made it to the bathroom. She showered and dressed and decided that a long walk in the fresh country air would do her the power of good. More importantly, there was something she needed to discuss with the Baron and she quickly thought of an excuse to return to his less-than-humble abode.

'I'm off to find out what's happened to Lydia,' she barked at James before slamming the bedroom door shut.

Once out of the hotel's grounds, Felicity stumbled around the Cotswold countryside until the golden gates leading to the Baron's extravagant home loomed before her. She marched straight up to the oak front door, beating it hard with the brass Welsh dragon shaped doorknocker. Almost immediately, the door was thrown wide open by the butler, allowing the sweet aroma of a carrot cake baking to escape into the frosty air.

'Helloo?' he enquired in his strange accent.

'Hello Dominic. I'd like to have a quick word with the Baron if that's at all possible?'

'And who may I ask is callin'?'

'You know very well who it is. It's Felicity Garrett. I was here last night and I'm positive that I met you at Meade Pullen's offices as well.'

Dominic reeled back jauntily in his green checked kilt.

'Yee'd better come in.'

The Baron was swiftly summoned and, as soon as he had straightened his "hair", led Felicity into a side room that she had not previously seen. It was decorated in pink, floral patterned wallpaper and furnished with very dated, worn sofas. Photographs of orange/brown-faced relatives stood on the mantelpiece.

'Do take a seat,' said the Baron, slightly ill at ease, sensing that Felicity had noticed that the décor was not at all in keeping with the rest of his splendid mansion. 'It was all the furniture that the Baroness would allow me to keep from my mam's 'ome in Bedwas,' he explained, slipping easily into his Welsh valleys accent, relieved that he no longer had to pretend to originate east of the Severn Bridge. 'We were very 'appy there,' he added. 'My twin brother and me spent many a day jumpin' on them settees.' The Baron ran his podgy little hand over the daffodil-decorated cushion cover. 'And my mam was forever knittin' socks for us and crochetin' hats sittin' just where you are now.' A tear ran down his face, causing a rivulet on his orange/brown skin.

Felicity took a deep breath. 'Coincidentally, it's your twin brother I'd like to speak to you about.'

'Who? Elwyn?'

'Yes, assuming that that's his forename. I only know him as Mr Roberts of Meade Pullen and Co.'

'Well, yes! I know them well. It's my Elwyn who keeps them buggers afloat. And I pay for all Roger's mistakes too. He's forever mucking up them claims.'

'I'm sorry to hear that.'

'Me too. Anyway, luv, how can I help you?' The Baron grew anxious. He glared at Felicity. 'I 'ope there's been no criticism of my wife's bakin' at the firm.'

'Not at all. It's just that I recently applied for a position at Meade Pullen and I was wondering if I might, cheekily,'

Felicity paused to lick her glossy lips, 'ask you to put in a good word for me?'

'Good God alive! Is that all? Of course! It would be no problem at all! For one moment I thought you might ask for my wife's secret carrot cake recipe and that, I'm afraid I would, naturally, have to refuse.'

'No, no. I'm quite set up in the cake department, thank you very much.' Felicity was always very proud of the elastic texture to her Victoria sponge.

The Baron breathed a sigh of relief. 'In that case, I'll get on the phone to Elwyn right away.'

Felicity thanked the Baron for his generous assistance with her career ambitions and then left swiftly, keen to avoid another awful episode at the Baron's home. By all accounts, she had got away lightly. On her way back down the long driveway she bumped into Lydia looking decidedly worse for wear without her glittery eyelashes and the one remaining "breast".

'Lydia, my goodness! Everything alright?' Stupid question, she thought immediately.

'Ugh! I feel gross. That Goddamn Baron put effing honey - thankfully it was organic - all over my arse and then emptied a feather pillow over me. He said he got a kick out of fucking chickens.'

'But what happened to your, um, bosom?'

'Don't ask.'

The two started walking back to the hotel together in silence. After a while Lydia looked down. 'He fried it.'

'Ah, I see.'

'I guess one's not much use to me anyway.'

'No. Probably not.' Felicity smiled to herself, glad to be a piscatorian.

Back at the hotel, Felicity returned to her bedroom whilst Lydia took a bath. James was still in bed when she opened the door and the sheets were draped over an upturned V shape above his groin.

'Oh do stop fiddling with yourself, James,' she ordered bossily from the doorway. 'It's so unnatural.' Since her future at Meade Pullen was now, apparently, sealed by courtesy of the Baron, she decided not to worry about being amiable to her annoying boyfriend any more.

'What else do you expect me to do? You're certainly not up for anything this morning.' Felicity snorted and began brushing her hair briskly into a ponytail. 'And,' she added glaring at his unshaven horizontal form in the reflection of the mirror, 'I can smell that you've been using my expensive lime, mandarin and basil body crème. That's very annoying, I must say, because I've only just bought it.' She pinched her thin nose between finger and thumb. 'Honestly, James, don't you remember the agony you were in last time you got it under your foreskin?'

James sat up in bed, placed a pillow over his citrus smelling groin and belched loudly in his round-vowelled voice. 'By the way,' he added off-handedly, the V shape fast disappearing, 'I think I should mention that Lydia told me that she saw you with Mark last night.'

'What do you mean?' Felicity froze; her well made plans rushing uncontrollably out of the window.

'She came to find me when I was in the kitchen with the Baroness.' James withdrew his hands from beneath the duvet, blushing brightly before continuing. 'It was really quite fascinating, you know, Fliss. She was showing me how to chop up carrots with only two fingers and a thumb on each hand.' He paused to flatten the bed cover. 'Actually it was a bit scary with all those knives flying about.' James snapped his fingers against each other like scissors to give a full demonstration of the previous night's scene. 'You know, she can dice two carrots at the same time?'

'Gosh! Really?'

'Yes!'

James, momentarily forgetting what they were supposed to be discussing, beamed at Felicity. He then glimpsed a small love bite on her neck and scowled, reverting to his earlier complaint. 'Lydia said that when she went to the wine cellar with the driver to do some tasting, she had to cross the courtyard in front of the music room and saw you through the window kissing Mark. Pity for you that the Baron's not keen on curtains.'

'Well,' Felicity snapped, her cheeks turning an uncharacteristic red. 'In fact, for your information, it was Mark who kissed me. Not me kissing Mark. And there's a world of difference.' Although dismayed to think that her plot might be going awry, she was pleased with her smart response. There was no way on earth, now she was so close to having her dreams of success in the city fulfilled, that she would be prepared to let them slip from her fingers, all ten of them, no less. It was also unthinkable that James might even consider dumping her. Perish the thought.

'Whatever.' James threw back the bed sheet, made his way to the bathroom and closed the door behind him.

Oh fuck, thought Felicity. She could hear James turning on the shower, pottering about as his performed his ablutions and went over to the window to look out over the rolling Cotswolds countryside. She needed some inspiration as to how to manage the situation that was unfolding horribly before her. She wasn't used to having to deal with a truculent James. He had clearly been having too much sex, she thought. All that letting off steam in inappropriate places meant that his usual polite, concerned nature had been blown away, puffed out into oblivion.

Felicity chewed the inside of her lip nervously before mustering up sufficient courage to gingerly open the bathroom door and allow steam to pour out. She padded in and stood on the bathmat.

'Look James,' she said. 'You've got to believe me. I pushed Mark away. I honestly don't find him attractive in the least. We were both drunk and he was trying his luck, that's all.'

James wiped some condensation from the shower glass and peered through it at Felicity. 'I really don't want to talk about this now, Fliss. I've got a whopper of a headache. Let's discuss it another time. OK?'

'Sure.' Felicity slowly backed out of the bathroom clutching the half-used toiletries. 'You know how fond I am of you,' she added, stuffing shampoo bottles into her case.

*

James, Felicity, Mark and Lydia finally arrived back in London late that Sunday afternoon. There had been a certain *froideur* amongst the occupants of the Land Cruiser as they travelled along the motorway and, as a result, Felicity hadn't had an opportunity to discuss personal matters with James. In any event, Felicity strongly believed that time was a great healer, and therefore decided to speak to him later in the week.

ELWYN

The following day, Elwyn Roberts stormed into Roger's office. 'I've had second thoughts about Felicity,' he yelled hysterically.

Roger casually flicked over a page of his fishing magazine before turning up his eyes to rest on his colleague's anxious face. 'I knew you'd come round to my way of thinking,' he said.

'Well, to cut a long story short, I have personal reasons for wanting her on our books and it has nothing to do with her supposed abilities as a lawyer, her pert backside, her delicate ankles or her crisp voice for that matter.'

Roger, surprised by Elwyn's unusually accurate observations, raised his eyebrows.

'Fine,' he said. 'I'll try to get hold of her.' He telephoned Felicity's mobile and left a message on her voice mail.

Roger had not looked at Sarah's telephone number, given to him by Geoffrey, since their meeting at the wine bar and decided to wait a few days more before calling. He hoped that Felicity would phone in the interim to accept the position with Meade Pullen partly because he wanted to spite the managing partner by incurring a recruitment agent's fee but mainly because of her wondrous ankles that made him feel dizzy. However, his telephone had remained silent for days. This was slightly worrying though not altogether unusual given his receptionist's abilities. Reluctantly, Roger opened his wallet and pulled out the crumpled piece of paper that Geoffrey had handed him. He dialled the number scribbled in biro on it and, after a couple of rings, Sarah answered.

'Ah, yes, hello. I'm terribly sorry to bother you, but I'm a friend of Geoffrey Carter QC and he's suggested that I call you. My name's Roger Wilbraham-Evans.'

'Oh yes?' Sarah's eyes bulged as she fought hard for breath, trying to zip up her trousers.

'Geoffrey tells me that you're looking to move from Portshires. Mentioned something about redundancies. I guess you'd like to jump before you're pushed, as they say.'

Sarah breathed out in relief as her stomach bulged over the trouser waistband.

'Actually, I've always hoped that I might make it to Meade Pullen one day and Mr Carter mentioned that you might be looking for an assistant.'

'Indeed we are. Any chance that you could come and meet me at the office? Just a very informal chat, nothing too serious. Next Monday suit you?'

'Yes, that would be fine but I'd have to come after work. Would six be too late?'

'Not at all,' Roger replied, running his eyes over the cover of *Fish Now!* 'I never leave before 6.30 anyway. Too much to do.'

Roger made a note in his diary of the meeting with Sarah before easing open the top left hand drawer of his polished mahogany desk. He pulled out a gold plated telephone, pressed only one digit and was immediately put through to Ty Bach. It was the direct line to the Baron's home.

After three rings the great man himself answered. 'Hello, Roger,' he said, sighing loudly. 'How much do you need this time, boyo?'

'Ah, Baron. Sorry to trouble you again, twice in one week, but we've just been struck out on another claim. No one's fault, *obviously*,'

'Obviously. It never is, is it, Roger?'

'Mmm. Anyway, the good news is that this one only involves a sprained wrist so we should be able to get away with a couple of grand. We missed a trial date, that's all.'

'So how much is that in trout terms?'

'A hundred?'

'Come, come, you'll have to do better than that. The Baroness eats at least ten a day and Dominic needs double that.'

'Two hundred then.'

'That's more like it. I'll put the cash in a parcel for Dominic to bring in tomorrow.' Roger heard the Baron whoop with glee as he played tiddly-winks with his gold coins.

'Baron, I don't know what we'd do with out you,' he said.

'Me neither. And you know, I don't mind our little arrangement at all, providing my twin brother doesn't find out.' The Baron paused for a second or two before continuing. 'Although I must admit the Baroness does whiff of fish a bit sometimes.'

The Baron shook his head, wrinkling up his orange/brown nose as he thought of his piscatorial wife and flicked a coin high into the air. He sat, transfixed, as he watched it land right in the middle of a plateful of rubies.

'And Elwyn is doing well, by the way,' Roger added politely, trying not to sob audibly as he recognised the tinkling sound of gold on gem. 'It was only the other day that he mentioned how much he was enjoying the carrot cake.'

'Oh, well. I'm pleased to hear that. The Baroness takes a lot of trouble over them beauties,' he added, slipping back into his voice from the Valleys. 'She pays particular attention to the soft icing so that it doesn't damage his dentures too much. I don't want to start paying out for any more replacement teeth, as well as all the rest.'

'Very wise, Sir, very wise.'

'Anyway, I'll let the Baroness know about the delivery. She'll be delighted.'

Roger put down the telephone and dug out his troutometer. He studied it carefully, calculating how many hours he would have to spend on the banks of his freezing pond to enable him to catch all those dratted fish. It was vital that he kept a close eye on his fast dwindling stocks of trout as it was only the secret deal he had with the Baron that was keeping Meade Pullen afloat.

'Bugger,' he said, and put the 'phone away.

SOUTHAMPTON

The following Thursday, Felicity sat in the meeting room at her firm's offices in Southampton taking a statement from the balding male client sitting opposite her. She found that she was experiencing grave difficulties in concentrating on Mr Hodge's dilemma and, acutely aware that sympathy was one of her weak points, realised that she would need to work hard on that facet of her personality if she was to progress her career as a caring, clinical negligence lawyer. Felicity stared blankly at Mr Hodge as she tried to work out what his complaint was all about.

'So,' she said crisply, trying hard to drag her mind away from thoughts of her daliance in the Cotswolds, 'do you really think that a delay of two hours in diagnosing a fractured arm made any difference to your recovery from a jet-ski accident?'

Felicity despised jet skis.

The man shook his head. 'Could have done. I might have died.'

'Sorry? What? You mean drowned?'

'No, no, no. Those doctors could have missed a brain tumour or something.'

'Do you have a brain tumour?'

'No.'

The client stopped talking for a minute and thought carefully about Felicity's question. 'But,' he said, his eyes brightening as his brain creaked into activity, 'the docs didn't check for one.'

'Mmm. But what has the slight delay in establishing that you had, in fact, fractured rather than bruised your forearm got to do with a brain tumour?' Felicity stared incredulously at her client, once again fighting back the urge to recall her entanglement with Mark.

'Well the point I'm trying to make, Miss, if you'd just let me speak, is that if they missed one thing, they could have missed a hundred. I could be crippled, you just never know.'

Felicity took a deep breath, demonstrating a tight-lipped smile to her vexatious client. 'The trouble with claiming compensation for personal injuries is that you are only allowed, in law, to recover damages for injuries that have actually occurred or are very, very likely to occur at some time in the future. Otherwise, your injuries and therefore damages would be endless and therefore not quantifiable.'

'Exactly.' Mr Hodge leaned forward again. 'That's what I've been trying to tell you, if you'd only listen. My injuries could well be endless. There's only him upstairs,' he pointed towards the false ceiling indicating that his god might be nestling somewhere amongst the recessed lights, 'and the lady who reads tea leaves down my road who can really prophesise. Not them quacks. You know, I read in The Mimphampton Gazette only the other day, that a man was awarded thirty grand after he fell over a broken pavin' slab. If that's so then I should get at least a million. I might never work again. That's me ruined.'

Atypically, Felicity was at a loss for words. She had already taken full stock of her client and, to her experienced eye, realised that she would need to use an enormous wedge of diplomacy to ensure there were no repercussions. This man looked just the type to complain about her to The Law Society.

'I'm terribly sorry, Mr Hodge, I couldn't possibly comment on any aspect of that case as I'm simply not familiar with the facts. The problem with your claim is twofold. Firstly, there is no evidence to suggest that the hospital staff were in any way in breach of their duty of care to you and, secondly, that you did in fact sustain any injury by such a breach even if, in fact, there was one. Essentially, what you're asking me to do is sue a publicly funded institution.' The client looked confused. 'The NHS,' she explained, 'for a brief delay between the taking of the X-ray and the Consultant Radiologist reporting on it.'

'I might get cancer from that X-ray.'

Felicity clenched her fingers tightly, just as her psychoanalyst had advised her to do on such occasions. Extreme violence crossed her mind.

'You know, Mr Hodge, you might just have a point there. And, as I'm feeling in such a generous mood today,' she continued, flashing her expensively straightened front teeth at the bewildered client, 'I'll take on your claim if you like, and, since you think you've got such a strong case, I'm willing to act on your behalf on a private basis. My hourly rate is £350 plus VAT, of course, and I generally expect my clients to place £1000 on account. Do you have your chequebook with you? Or are you a man who prefers to deal in cash?'

Mr Hodge blinked. He gulped hard, his epiglottis bulging out of his neck excitedly as he stood up, tipping his chair backwards. This was definitely not what he had been expecting, Felicity thought, pleased with her tactics to rid herself of such a tiresome man.

'Having thought long and hard about my claim,' he replied, reaching for his jacket, 'I'm not quite sure what I'll be doing. As you know, I'm not interested in the money, it's the point in principle that concerns me.' Felicity managed to stifle a laugh. 'But,' he added as he swung his jacket casually over his shoulder. 'If I do decide to take it further, I'll definitely be in touch.'

Felicity was delighted with her impressive ability to dismiss a potential client and returned to her desk to check her In-box. She scrolled down the entries. There was a mass of garbage about office protocol from the Practice Manager that she instantly deleted, but nothing from James. She hadn't heard from him since the weekend and was beginning to regret being so mean to him, particularly about his weight problem. It was the only thing he had ever really worked hard at in his whole life, she realised, and perhaps she ought to respect him for that? She walked over to the window and looked out. It was make or break time, she thought. She either stayed in Southampton and finished with James or moved in with him. The latter would mean a sideways career step and was not something that she was overly keen to contemplate. On the other hand, she simply couldn't continue with her half-lives in both places. More positively, might she meet someone more suitable in London? Somebody, yes somebody, like Jeremy Paxman. The answer was obvious. She found James' e-mail address, typed in the words "I love you" and pressed the send button.

That should do the trick.

TARA

After being interviewed by Roger and John (who, as the most senior assistant solicitor in the firm, had stepped in at the last minute when Marina had had to leave the office unexpectedly, muttering incoherently about doughnuts), Sarah made her way along Gray's Inn Road and called her sister.

'Hi, it's me!' she chirped, a little too shrilly for Tara's hungover state.

'Ugh. Oh yeah. How'd it go?' Tara slurred into her mobile phone. She hung on tightly to the diamante necklace her sister had given to her as a birthday gift, hoping to balance herself.

'Really well!'

Tara's puffy eyelids began to close as she stood in a doorway, swaying gently whilst her sister gabbled on.

'It was more of, well, a chat, than an interview,' continued Sarah. 'It was just with one of the partners and another solicitor. Can't remember his name but I thought he was bit of a pushy guy, in fact.'

'Right, right,' muttered Tara, irritated by her sister's jolly voice. 'So have they offered you a job, or what?'

'Well,' said Sarah launching off into detail, 'the situation is that they're waiting to hear from some other solicitor in Southampton who they've already offered the position to but I definitely got the impression that they might consider me, if she doesn't accept.'

'So, what next?'

'They're going to call her - Fiona, I think her name is - tomorrow and give her until the end of the week to make a decision. Hopefully, by this time next week I'll be able to tell Portshires where to stick their crummy job.'

Tara suddenly realised that her stomach was about to make an overt demonstration of anger at having too much cheap wine hurled into it.

'Gotta go,' she muttered. 'Not feeling too bright.' She clicked off her mobile and vomited onto the pavement. Tara may well have been an employee of the British Broadcasting Corporation but when push came to shove she could happily puke outside a police station without too much compunction.

Sarah replaced her handset and thought back to the interview. She had found Mr Wilbraham-Evans receptive to her grin-at-every-comment foible but John Forrester's demeanour harder to gauge. The questions he had asked her were bizarre. Why on earth would he have wanted to know what her ideal holiday would be and how she liked to spend her Saturday nights? Surely the position was for an assistant solicitor and not a travel rep? Still, since she wanted the job so badly, she was prepared to accommodate even the strangest of interviewers. More worrying, though, was the array of photographs lining the hall. Who was the strange Cub Scout gorging on sausages and who was the woman dressed in what looked like a nightie gobbling up fish?

*

As the days passed, Felicity grew increasingly concerned about not hearing anything from James. She fretted that her dalliance with Mark had pushed him too far; that being labelled a cuckold was more than he could bear and that he no longer wished to see her. Felicity knew full well that his years spent at a rural Boarding School had taught him to be long-suffering but that there was, understandably, a limit to his patience. Once, he had been suspended for a week for trying to smuggle in some extra croissants after being placed on a strict diet. If he could be that defiant, goodness only knew what he would do about her tussle with the marvellous buttocks of his closest, so-called friend. Felicity lay in bed becoming uncommonly tearful as she recalled James' familiar flabby jaw line and eyes that were too close together.

On the other hand, she thought, perking up, in a strange sort of way she was grateful to Lydia for telling James about the little episode between her and Mark at the Baron's home as it had, effectively, resulted in her positively reassessing her relationship with him. In fact, Lydia's spiteful intentions had inadvertently made her realise just how kind and patient James was and Felicity had finally come to appreciate just how desperate Lydia was to remain living with James and to have him for herself. Either way, though, she strongly regretted paying for her makeover at the Copse House Hotel; she should have let her spend the weekend looking like an Afghan hound.

Felicity sat at her desk at work and despite trying to concentrate on an expert's report she found herself re-reading sections over and over again. Not the most riveting of stuff even at the best of times but she did like to make the effort. She even considered, in her desperation, contacting the dreadful Mr Hodge to see if he had decided to pursue his claim.

Later that evening, bored with extensively examining the intricacies of her face in the mirror, Felicity decided to take the plunge and called James' flat. Lydia answered the telephone.

'Hi. Ching Wong's Chinese Takeaway. May I take your order please?'

'Lydia, it's Felicity. Is James there please?'

'Wong number. This is a lestaulant. You must oldel.'

'Enough, Lydia. Could you get James for me, please?'

'Can't,' she explained, reverting to her middle-England accent. 'He's in the Chelsea and Westminster Hospital. Has been since Monday.'

'What?'

'Yep. The day after we got back from Copse House Hotel he sort of collapsed and was rushed in by ambulance. Didn't you notice how quiet he was?'

'Yes, I did!' Felicity gasped. 'But I thought it was just because he was cross with me. Is he alright?'

'Yeah, yeah. He'll be out tomorrow. They just had to do some tests, that's all.'

'What tests? What's wrong with him?'

'Nothing. It was just because he was on that silly diet. His body couldn't deal with the egg overload. Anyway, the hospital slop, I mean food, was so grim that not even James could be tempted. In some ways you might say that the diet was, after all, quite successful. I don't think he'll be wanting an omelette for a few months though.'

'Oh my goodness! I'll be up tomorrow evening after work. Could you let him know?'

'I'll do my best.' Lydia hung up.

The next day, as promised, Felicity went to James' flat. James, very pale and much thinner, though still pushing some sixteen stones, opened the front door and engulfed her with his loose-skinned arms.

'My love, how good to see you.' Felicity buried her head against his ample chest. 'I've been so worried!' she cried out, gagging on his matted chest hair. 'Why didn't you call me?'

'The sister in charge of the ward confiscated my mobile the moment I was admitted. None of the phones worked and so I asked Lydia to call you. She did, didn't she?'

'No!' Felicity said crossly. 'Well, she might have called me on my mobile but I left it in the back of your parents' car. Didn't you spot it when you were unpacking? And the phone in the flat has been quiet as a mouse all week.' Felicity gulped, making a strange toad-like noise in her throat. 'I've been out of my mind, James.'

A lone tear welled up in her left eye that she quickly wiped away on James' sweater. 'I thought you had dumped me.'

'What? Because of Mark? Don't be silly. I know what he's like. I just felt too rough to speak on the way back and, to be honest, I had quite a fright being in that dark kitchen with the Baroness.' James looked at Felicity with drooping eyes, hoping for sympathy. 'She must have been quite a gal in her time, you know. Can't quite work out why she wanted to stick her finger up my bum, though,' he added, shaking his head in disbelief. 'Don't think she was looking for piles.'

ROGER

'Hello? Could you put me through to Mr Wilbraham-Evans, please Dominic?'

'Helloo? Yes, certainly. May I tek yur nem?'

'It's Felicity. Felicity Garrett.'

'Putting yu thru.'

A strange rummaging noise followed, as if someone was searching for a crisp packet in a bin.

'Hulloo?' he asked again.

'Yes?'

'Ah'm having a wee problem finding Mr Wilbraham-Evans. Could ah tek yur number and ask him to get back to yer?'

Felicity gave Dominic the requested details. It was Thursday and by the end of the working day Roger had not returned her call.

In the meantime, John Forrester decided that he was going to take the matter of the new appointee into his own hands. He sat in his room, scratching his head and pushing sheets of paper across his desk, when it slowly dawned on him that both in the office and in his own home he held no authority. He was a frustrated soul; after ten years' of drudging, day after day, to the offices of Meade Pullen and Co, and, after ten years of scorn from his vicious wife, he was still only an associate solicitor. In fact, thinking back, even on their wedding night, his wife had made it abundantly clear that she had planned on marrying a successful lawyer, not a scruffy dimwit who ambled along in life. She wanted change and she wanted a man who had slicked back hair and round glasses; someone who would roll up his newspaper up neatly once he had read it from cover to cover and have hearty chats with their neighbours as they cut their respective lawns on a sunny summer's day. What sort of a man, she demanded, could continue to return home year after year without his name being emblazoned on the firm's notepaper as proof of partnership? Worse still, what sort of a man allowed females to boss him about at work?

The final straw had been when his wife threatened that only an improvement in his status would halt her unrelenting torment. Only then would she cease putting steel tacks in the soles of his shoes to prick his feet as he ambled along.

*

John sat at his desk examining his shoes, thinking long and hard about the two applicants. Sarah had appeared to be a happy-go-lucky type of girl whom he thought might prove useful to him in due course. Judging from what he had seen on paper she was the ideal type to manipulate; her exam grades were adequate but mediocre. As for looks, she was plain; someone with whom he could socialise without incurring any wrath from his wife. More importantly, she was someone who would never be a threat to his career. John was next in line for promotion and this time he didn't want anyone or anything to stand in his way.

However, the only issue that was slightly in Felicity's favour was the fact that she had a notice period of only one month whereas Sarah's was three months'. Some of the files to be handed over hadn't been worked on for months and, if the ire of The Law Society was to be avoided, someone was needed to sort out those files double quick.

*

John walked up the wide staircase to Roger's office. He ignored the gold-plated plaque stating that Mr Wilbraham-Evans was "out", knocked on the door and, without waiting for a reply, entered.

'Come in!' Roger squawked from behind numerous mounds of files perched precariously on his desk. 'Do take a seat on the banquette,' the voice continued. John hesitated, tutting loudly. He hated sitting on that dratted piece of furniture; his short legs made it impossible for him to sit comfortably in the deep faux leather seat. He perched himself on the banquette's sharp edge so that his bottom was halved laterally and placed his left elbow awkwardly on the high armrest for support.

'Look, Roger,' he said, shifting about uncomfortably, alternately easing the pressure from one buttock to the other. 'I need to discuss the appointment of the new solicitor with you. I assume you haven't heard from that Felicity Garrett girl yet?'

'No, surprisingly. I can only assume that she's had a better offer.' Roger sighed and scratched his head, ruffling a few strands of his thick hair before slowly moving some of the larger files off his desk and on to the carpet. 'She's got damn fine ankles, you know,' he said solemnly after a long pause. Roger stood up and walked towards the large window, clearly in some dismay. 'It would be a shame if she didn't join us.'

John thought of his own wife's legs, always clad in the thickest of cloth to stop mortal man from glimpsing her hairy, muscle bound thighs. 'Really?' he said. 'I'm not so sure about that. The other girl seemed pretty keen. I actually preferred her.'

'Did you?' asked Roger, flabbergasted. 'I'm afraid she didn't spark any fires in me. Not my type at all. Felicity, on the other hand... well...' he gazed dreamily out across Gray's Inn Road as visions of his choice of assistant suffused his mind. 'She was something special.'

Silence reigned as John, momentarily forgetting that he was far too short to lean back into the great expanse of leather, found himself suddenly horizontal on the senior partner's couch. Rather embarrassed, he struggled to sit upright, his legs sticking out parallel to the floor.

'Can I help you, John?' asked Roger, clearly concerned about his employee's predicament.

'No, no. Quite alright now.' 'Sir', he almost added, but stopped himself before deference got the better of him.

'Realistically,' Roger continued, gloomily, 'if I don't hear from Felicity, by close of play tomorrow afternoon, why don't you give Sarah a call? Then the job's hers, if she wants it, of course,' he added, crossing his fingers behind his back as he spoke. That big lump of a girl really didn't do anything to raise his morale, he thought gloomily and glanced over at the telephone, urging it to ring.

'At least that way it will give Felicity another full working day to respond.'

'Great. I'll do that.' John's eyes brightened at the thought of a golden opportunity. He inched his way slowly off the banquette. 'I think that's a sensible idea, Roger.' John sauntered out of the room, smiling to himself as he made his way back to his pokey office.

*

That evening, in Fulham, Felicity cooked supper for James. As a general rule, she tended to stay out of the kitchen since departing from medical college, as it was there that she seemed to experience the majority of the frightening flashbacks to her student days. In particular, she found that grilling fish produced the same smell that floated away from the operating theatre following a haemorrhoidectomy. Cauterised flesh. Felicity gasped. Her conversation with James when he informed her of the Baroness' attempt at foreplay had stirred something in her cerebral cortex. The twinkly-eyed Professor of Surgery loomed above the hob, floating on a bed of Cos lettuce.

James was extremely sympathetic to this unfortunate condition and, as a general rule, managed to keep Felicity clear of any culinary activity. However, as a gesture of goodwill in the light of the "Mark in the Music Room" episode, Felicity felt obliged to make his favourite dish - seared tuna, knowing that "egg" was still a dirty word.

Fortunately, there was only a minimum of actual cooking involved, as James had wisely purchased ready-prepared salad and garlic bread to accompany their meal. He had lain out all the ingredients on the granite counter and all Felicity had to do was to quickly fry the fish. She carefully placed the griddle on the gas flame to heat up and, a few slugs of wine later, the tuna steaks were thrown in to cook. All was well.

'Everything alright, Fliss?' James asked solicitously from his chair in the living room.

'Yes thanks.'

Felicity wiped her hands, now clammy with anticipation, on her apron and prepared to remove the steaks from the heat. She grasped the griddle handle with one hand and the spatula with the other and carefully inspected the fish. They were just right. Quite pink. Perfect.

As the steaks were being transported to the supper plates, the whiff of cooking meat, albeit fish, caught her nostrils. Felicity sniffed.

'Oh, Lord, not again!' she wailed, feeling the imminent approach of a flashback. She held her breath in anticipation. Too late. It had already arrived. The flashback hit home with full force.

'They'll never return after one of my special branding sessions.' The Prof, as he liked to be called, had smugly informed her after a particularly unpleasant display of dexterity. Felicity's hand trembled as she thought back to her days spent at the medical college. Those old-fashioned procedures did seem to work, she accepted. She swallowed hard. Her heart rate slowed but it was all too late. The tuna steaks left the griddle, fluttered delicately through the kitchen air as if some Act of God was returning them to the deep blue sea and then hovered in slow motion before finding their final resting place on the linoleum floor.

'Oh, shit!' Felicity cried out. James leapt to his feet as his worst fears were being realised.

'Fliss? What's happened?'

'Nothing, nothing.' Felicity shut the kitchen door quickly. 'Don't come in. I'm just putting the garnish on.' Felicity scooped up the tuna, now crumbled into pieces, slapped them cruelly onto the plate and threw a few uncooked runner beans on top. 'Ta da!' she exclaimed as she presented the dishes to James a few moments later. 'It's tuna nicoise. I thought it might be nice to have a change.'

'Good idea,' said James picking up his fork. 'What is it they say? Ah yes, 'A change is as good as a rest'. Yes, that's it.' He started munching on a runner bean. 'And nouvelle cuisine as well, I see!' Felicity smiled coyly. 'You *are* a clever Fliss!' James enthused, once again. 'And I thought, stupidly, *obviously*, that you were having one of your turns.'

'Ha, ha! No, no!' Felicity poured out more wine. 'Eat up!' The couple sat in silence as James tried to decipher what, exactly, his supper was made of.

'So, Fliss,' he said brightly as he tore apart some garlic bread. (He was on safe ground there, he thought wisely.) 'What do you fancy doing tomorrow? I'm still on sick leave so we should make the most of it, you know.'

'How about Tate Modern?' proposed Felicity. She had had her eye on visiting the Edward Hopper exhibition ever since she had seen an article written by A.A.Gill, who, thought Felicity, was a suitor comparable to the marvellous Paxman. Subsequently, should she ever bump into A.A.Gill at some literary festival, or wherever (at a glamorous book launch, *peut etre*), they would have something in common to discuss and a relationship would, undoubtedly, flourish therefrom.

'Super idea. We'll go first thing. Maybe we could have breakfast on the way?' James suggested, quite certain that he would be ravenous in the morning.

'Yes, I guess we could do but I'd like to drop in to Meade Pullen at some point. You know, it's strange that Mr Wilbraham-Evans hasn't called me back. I rather got the impression that he was quite keen on me.' Felicity shrugged her shoulders. 'Maybe not.' She popped a fork full of crumbled tuna into her mouth, chomped hard for longer than she had anticipated, gulped, and continued. 'I'd like to get the job situation over by the weekend so that we can sort out a place to live.' Felicity fell silent as she heard

Lydia opening the front door. She leaned forward towards James to speak in a hushed voice. 'The sooner you're out of here, the better.'

James didn't reply. He chewed on, regardless.

*

The following day, as planned, Felicity nipped up the now familiar steps to the entrance of Meade, Pullen and Co. She raised her hand to rattle the front door just as it was thrown open by Mr Wilbraham-Evans.

'Hello!' he said, beaming at her broadly. Roger stepped down onto the pavement as the door slammed shut behind him. 'Oh, bother,' he muttered, turning and peering through the grubby glass. 'Were you coming in to see me?'

'Yes, actually,' replied Felicity. 'I've called a number of times but I haven't managed to get past the receptionist. I assumed you must have been out of the office on business.'

'Oh, no,' said Roger, appalled (at the idea of business). 'Actually, just between you and me,' he paused to look suspiciously over his shoulder before he continued, 'we've got a bit of a problem with our receptionist at the moment.'

'Oh?'

'Mmm. Likes a bit of a tipple. Between meals, if you know what I mean.' He tipped his right thumb and forefinger to his lips to give a full illustration of the predicament. Felicity raised a knowledgeable eyebrow in response, wondering, for half a second, why the driver/butler/receptionist should depart from his usual cake and trout consummation. How on earth would he have time, or more pertinently, the internal space, to imbibe all this fluid on top of all the fish? Roger, meanwhile, mistook her wide-eyed expression for flirtation and, most flattered, beamed at her again as he recalled her lower limbs.

'So,' he said, rubbing his hands and wiggling his lithe hips in anticipation, 'have you made a decision about our offer?'

Felicity confirmed her acceptance.

'Ah, wonderful!' Roger lunged forward to gather Felicity's hands in his own and, for one awful moment, she thought he was going to swing her up into the air.

'Look,' he said, still hanging on to her wrists, 'I'm off to buy a sandwich. Cheese and pickle probably. Could I tempt you with one, too? Maybe you're more of a brie and cranberry girl? Would that suit you better, perhaps?'

'Thanks, but no. I'm off to the Tate Modern now. There's an exhibition on that I've been hoping to see for some time.'

'Yes, of course. Lots to do in Southwark now. You could walk over that wobbly bridge. Should only take you about twenty minutes from here. We're not that far away from civilisation in Gray's Inn Road as some might think, you know. Still plenty happening around Chancery Lane, I hear.'

'Yes, I…' Felicity mumbled as she unsuccessfully attempted to participate in the conversation.

'I'm far too old for that kind of thing now, but, in my heyday, well…ha,ha!' Roger finally quietened down as sweet memories of his youth returned. He looked into the middle distance, his eyes narrowing as visions of short-skirted lawyers, both male and female filled his mind. 'Oh, yes!' he breathed passionately.

'Mr Wilbraham-Evans?' Felicity asked nervously.

'Sorry?' Roger replied, rejoining the land of the living. 'Where were we? Ah, yes. You're accepting the position. Marvellous.'

'When would you like me to start?'

'Could you speak to Marina about that? She's good at sorting out that technical stuff. But let me know if you have any problems.'

With that, Roger wandered off to the sandwich shop, waving his right hand at her over his shoulder. Felicity stood on the steps for a few moments watching her prospective employer before setting off to meet James, thoughts of a meeting with A.A. Gill filling her mind.

*

Ten minutes later, Roger returned to his office, freshly prepared sandwich in hand. Having moved some of the larger files off his brimming desk and onto the floor, he sat down, opened up his newspaper and began making his way through his lunch; cheese and pickle on wholemeal with a mere whisper of butter. He had had the same sandwich every day for the past ten years; never wavering except on one occasion when, feeling particularly frivolous, he had ventured into the land of bacon. An afternoon of the most indescribable indigestion, however, had reassured him that he should never return.

Apart from the sandwich incident, Roger was a very content man. He married late to a divorcee, named Pamela, who had two grown-up children from her former marriage. He even got on well with Pamela's ex-husband to the extent that they went on many a summer cruise around the Baltics with the ex and his new, much younger, slimmer wife. Evidently, she was a more youthful version of the gracious Pamela and it pleased Roger to see what an attractive woman his wife used to be.

Roger finished his sandwich and decided to nip out to the newsagents to purchase the latest copy of *Fish Now!* He had spent most of his earnings as an equity partner on developing a trout farm on the land surrounding his house outside the small market town of Buckingham and had spent a small fortune (or so Pamela informed her friends at the golf club) on building a lake to house the trout and then equipping it with enough fish to ensure that he never failed to be successful on each and every fishing expedition. And what expeditions they were! Even though Roger only had to walk a few hundred yards to reach his lake, he would always start off early in the morning, before daybreak, cheese and pickle sandwich prepared by the lovely Pamela the day before, in hand, and enough fishing equipment to supply eight fishermen. Then, by the murky depths of the pond, he would wait patiently until his hands were roused into action by the nibble of a trout at the end of his rod and would only leave when his plastic bucket was filled to the brim with thrashing fish. Oh, Joy of Joys! How Roger longed for those days as he sat in his stuffy office, listening to the secretaries typing sporadically on their Royal typewriters.

Never in all the time it had taken him to dig out the pond had he envisaged having to barter with his precious trout to keep the firm afloat. He shook his head as he thought of the beauties he had just parted with in return for payment from the Baron for yet another of his numerous litigious mistakes. This time it was for the late service of a Claim Form. Honestly! The fuss the Defendants had made just because he was a day late! *Fashionably* late, as he had advised them before they threw the Form back into his smiling face. Well, he thought, there had been simply no alternative but to strike another deal with the Baron and he felt he should be grateful that the Baroness had the remarkable ability to consume such vast quantities of trout. It was abundantly clear that she was addicted to its apparent age-reducing qualities and Roger had nearly fallen over when he learnt that she was 83 years old. She was also *fantastic* at front crawl.

*

Roger swept the breadcrumbs from his V-necked blue jersey and, after a lot of searching, eventually found his wallet tucked into one of the files on his desk. He stood up and, as he strode across the room, a very flustered John Forrester flung open the door.

'Hi, Roger,' he panted. 'Sorry to bother you but I wanted to let you know that I've spoken to Sarah Kelleher.'

'Oh, really?'

'Yes!' John squawked in an overly excited tone. 'And she's accepted our offer! She'll hand in her notice today. In fact,' he said, looking at his watch, 'she's probably already done so. She'll be starting here in three months' time.'

Roger turned pale. 'Oh, Lord,' he said, aghast. 'Felicity Garrett has accepted as well. I saw her about an hour ago. Hell. What do we do now? We'll have increased the number of female solicitors by two hundred percent. Messrs Meade and Pullen,' he said waving his hand through the musty air, 'will be turning in their graves.' He pulled at his thick head of hair, looking searchingly at John's wobbling, round face.

'I'm so sorry, Roger.' John ran a stubby finger around the inside of his collar. 'I really thought I was doing the right thing by calling her this morning. I was worried that she might leave the office early on a Friday. Isn't that what these female solicitors do? Don't they get their hair blow-dried or go shopping or something? I didn't want to miss her.'

'Evidently.' Roger fought hard to stop his mind meandering back to *Fish Now!* 'Look,' he said trying to get a grip on this irksome situation. 'There's not much we can do about it. Fortunately, they both seem like pleasant girls. You'll have to make sure they've got enough to do, though.'

'Of course, of course. By the time Sarah starts, I'm sure I'll have thought of plenty. Felicity can deal with the urgent stuff.'

'Excellent. Well, that's another little drama sorted.'

Roger picked up his wallet and strode out of the office, leaving his assistant solicitor standing, pigeon toed and alone, in the room. John hung his head low. Had he blown his chances of partnership next year by being so impetuous, he asked himself? He crossed to the window and watched Roger prance across the road to reach the newsagents. He sighed loudly. It really was so annoying, he thought crossly to himself, that his future lay in the hands of a dandy. He needed a plan of action. He needed to eat some cake.

BRIGADIER AND
MRS ANTHONY PETERS

After a cultured weekend, mostly spent battling with herself over the Paxman/Gill debate, and in particular, over whom she considered to be the more attractive suitor, Felicity travelled back to Southampton. She uncharacteristically indulged herself by sleeping in late that Monday morning before traipsing into work and handing in her notice to the smirking partners, none too careful to hide their jubilant faces.

Strangely, thought Felicity as she sat at her desk, she might actually miss the offices in Southampton; she was beginning to like the android lawyers with whom she worked and it was only now that she was leaving that she had time to take note of the intricacies of her surroundings. It was, considered Felicity, as if her male co-workers had been moulded from the same template; their height ranged between 5'8' to 5'10', they wore their brown hair cut short, petrified into straight, spiky lines by the vigorous application of hair gel; round spectacles protected small, piggy eyes and highly polished, black shoes reflected their worried faces.

Occasionally, and only if the wearer were feeling particularly risqué, would they depart from the standard blue shirt always tucked into their y-fronts to prevent any undesirable escape and flaunt, unwisely, some might say, a striped one, instead. Generally, these quiet, virginal men lived peacefully at home with their parents without being under any threat of catching venereal disease.

These men were good lawyers.

*

Felicity sat on her bed feeling rather smug that she was moving to, quite possibly, the only vaguely interesting firm of solicitors in England. During one of many tortuous sessions, her psychoanalyst had suggested that she indulge in some occasional erotica to loosen her up and, with the exception of Marina Johannson, whose gender could lie anywhere between the poles, she was hoping that there would be little asexuality at Meade Pullen. Admittedly, there were a number of members of staff whom she had yet to meet but, even whilst walking around the office behind Marina, she was sure that she had sniffed an air of promiscuity, Roger being a prime example, of course.

Felicity's eyelashes fluttered as she imagined an improvement in her sex life away from James' loving arms and, more importantly, the increase in her salary. Salary? Felicity sat up straight. 'Shit!' She realised with a jolt that she had omitted to deal with the very significant subject of payment and as soon as she reached work the next morning she picked up the 'phone and dialled the number for Meade Pullen.

'Hello? Mr Wilbraham-Evans?'

'Felicity, dear girl,' he replied. 'Do call me Roger. We're all friends here, you know.'

'Right. Yes. Will do. I'm terribly sorry to trouble you, Mr, er, Roger. I did try to speak to Marina, as you suggested, but I understand that she's not in the office today.'

'Mmm. That's right. Chipped nail varnish in urgent need of attention. Something worrying like that. Anyway, what can I do to help?'

'Well,' said Felicity. 'I'm not sure where to start and you know, Roger, this is very embarrassing for me to ask, but I really need to know how much my salary will be.'

'Oh, yes? What's the going rate for assistant solicitors these days? I'm never quite sure. Thirty five, forty thousand? You probably know better than me. Forty five thousand? Does that sound about right?'

This sum being over £10,000 more than she was currently earning, it sounded very right.

'Oh, I see.' Felicity sniffed, sensing that there might be more in the pot. 'I had hoped, what with London weighting and so on,' she paused to give full effect to her cause, 'that it might be a little higher.'

'Ah,' replied Roger, momentarily distracted by thoughts of trout bait.

'You see, Roger,' Felicity sighed heavily as she spoke, preparing herself to tinker with the truth, 'I have to be one hundred percent certain that this move is right for me before I hand in my notice.'

'Quite right. Well, how about £48,000 then?'

Felicity stifled a little squeak of pleasure. 'That should be fine,' she replied. 'I'll inform the partners here of my plans, immediately.'

'So, you'll be here by the end of next month?'

'Absolutely. Can't wait.' Felicity paused and then added breathily: 'Thanks for sorting everything out, Roger. I hated having to ask you.'

'Not a problem at all, my dear. I quite understand.' That girl was far too attractive to be haggling over figures, except her own, Roger chuckled to himself.

*

Four weeks later, James drove down to Southampton to help move Felicity's belongings. After spending a night in the flat, they crammed Felicity's clothes into the back of James' parents' Land Cruiser. A £20 note was left in the pot in the kitchen to contribute to the cost of the cracked toilet seat: James' efforts - the egg diet was still taking its toll - and the pair drove north back to civilisation. Once outside James' flat, they parked the car and walked up to the front door. They hadn't been able to find any suitable accommodation to rent and so there had been no alternative but to remain in Fulham 'It's so 1980's! I can't bear it!' complained Felicity to her mother who still wore flares and had no idea what her daughter was talking about, assuming that cramped feet must be affecting her brain.

As they approached, the front door was thrown open by Lydia's friend, Jasper, just as James was placing his key in the lock.

'Hello! Do come in! Don't mind the mess!' he said wafting, stubbly faced, through the living room. 'We're just about to clear up after last night. Had a bit of a party.'

As Felicity stood in the hallway, she could just about hear Lydia's giggle emanating from the living room. She took a deep breath of the alcohol-filled air and, after following James through the doorway, discovered Lydia reclining on the gold sofa dressed solely in one of her own t-shirts. Even more horrifying was the fact that she was smoking a cigarette and knocking ash into a half-finished bowl of cereal.

Felicity seethed. She stomped over to the sash window, throwing it open to allow beer fumes to seep out into the rain and then peered more closely at the remainder of Lydia's breakfast. She choked at the sight before her. The cereal was her own dear muesli, specially prepared from organic ingredients. Those raisins, now smothered in ash and about to be carelessly tipped onto the floor, had been hand picked by Welsh Patagonians. It was pure sacrilege! She stomped out of the living room and down the hallway to James' bedroom. Felicity shook with rage. Could that girl sink much lower, she asked herself?

Felicity plonked her handbag onto James' crumpled duvet and immediately noticed a very obvious red wine stain on the new percale sheets. She reached under the pillow on her side of the bed but, instead of finding her cotton nightdress, she drew out a pair of black y-fronts with the initials JV hand embroidered onto the front. Felicity cried out hysterically, like a desperate housewife faced with a head of nits, on seeing such lavish underwear and reeled backwards, tripping over the vegetable rack. Earthy organic tubers were strewn everywhere. 'Not my carrots too!' she moaned, picking herself up.

Felicity scrambled to her feet and gathered up Jasper's pants. She carried them at arm's length back into the living room and threw them hastily onto the floor.

'James,' she said. 'We're leaving. This place and its inhabitants are revolting.'

Felicity stormed out of the flat, slamming the front door behind her, the sound of Lydia's shrill chortling still ringing in her ears. She was livid. Did Lydia have any idea whatsoever how long it had taken her to get the right balance of raisins to oats to create the perfect muesli, she asked herself? That cereal was like an only child to her; nurtured beyond belief.

After a few minutes of solitary torment, James hopped in the car and looked at her kindly, desperately hoping that her tear-stained, blotchy face wasn't permanent.

'Worry not, Fliss,' he said authoritatively. 'I've tried calling my parents to see if it's OK for us to stay with them for a few days,'

'What did they say?'

'Well, I'm afraid there was no reply.' James paused to hand Felicity his crumpled handkerchief. 'I guess they must be out having a walk or something but I'm sure it won't be a problem if we just turn up. Thankfully, Father has become much more relaxed as of late,' he added, popping his trusty sunglasses onto his head. 'I've got keys for their house, anyway, so we can just let ourselves in and get settled.'

Felicity dabbed at her swollen eyes, trying hard to smile through pinched lips as James yanked vigorously at the ignition. 'You know, James,' she said after they had jerked their way out onto the Fulham Road, their seatbelts straining at their chests. 'That Lydia makes my blood boil.'

James sighed wearily. 'Oh Fliss,' he replied, mounting the kerb. 'You mustn't let her bother you like that, you'll only end up having another turn.'

Felicity sniffed, pulling her sleeve up over her hand and dabbing pathetically at her nose. 'I know, I know. It was just the thought of that dreadful Jasper inserting my organic vegetables - you know how much they mean to me - into someone else's and undoubtedly his own, well, *den*, that made me mad.' A tear ran down her cheek. 'At least we'll get some peace and quiet at your parents'.'

'Absolutely,' shouted James above the noise of the squealing engine. 'Although I'm sure that Lydia was only feeding the carrots to her gerbils. Nothing for you to get that upset about. And I really don't think that Jasper could be bothered with them either. He's really not that keen on eating any fibre.'

Felicity rolled her eyes at the ceiling. Yet again, fools surrounded her. At that moment, though, her thoughts were interrupted by James changing gear whilst simultaneously glancing, rather recklessly, at his watch.

'Cheer up, Fliss,' he said. 'It's just after six so how about we pop in to *The Anglesea* on the way?'

Felicity agreed, thinking that a spritzer might calm her down and that James' penchant for devouring salt and vinegar crisps would render him speechless. That way, at least she would get a bit of peace and quiet, albeit for a short while.

They stopped at the pub and sat on the wooden benches outside, shivering occasionally in the gusting wind that threw dirt from the street into their eyes. James' attempts at contacting his parents had been fruitless but regardless of this and after a couple of drinks they decided to continue on to James parents' place situated on the smarter side of Bedford Park, in time for supper. They drew up into the gravelled driveway, as always freshly groomed by James' father, parked the car and then rang the doorbell. There was no reply.

'Look, James,' said Felicity. 'They must be in. The lights are on upstairs.' She squinted at the first floor windows, searching for signs of life. 'And I think I can see something flickering on and off in your parents' bedroom. Maybe they're watching television?'

'Mmm. They might be.' James knocked hard on the door. 'But I'm pretty sure that Father doesn't allow any viewing above ground level.' He scanned the bedroom's bay window and, still failing to get a response, began feverishly beating the doorknocker, clearly concerned for his parents' welfare.

'James, didn't you say you had keys?' Felicity asked, seeing shards of blue paint fly up into the night sky. James fished around in his jacket pocket. 'Oh, yes,' he replied. 'Here they are.' With a quick twiddle of the lock, the dark blue front door swung open and they stepped into a panelled hallway.

'Hello?' James called out. There was no reply. He called again, nervously searching the rooms for evidence of a break-in but the décor was as tidy as ever; the Peters' shoes were lined up against the wall in ascending size and the Sunday newspapers had been stacked neatly on the glass coffee table. Nothing appeared to be untoward.

As James turned on the hall lights a faint ruffling sound could be heard on the floor above them. A few moments later, James' father, Brigadier Anthony Peters, marched down the stairs clad only in a red, silk paisley dressing gown.

'Dad? Everything alright?'

'Hello, James, my boy. Yes, of course everything's all right. I was just about to have a shower, that's all,' he explained. 'Mum's, um, resting.'

'What? At seven o' clock in the evening? I thought she'd be getting your supper ready.'

'No, not tonight. Never on a Sunday. We're having a few friends round this evening and she's just having a lie down before the party kicks off.'

James looked around and noticed that there was a distinct lack of canapés and the like that were usually associated with socialising. However, unperturbed, he continued. 'I was just wondering if it might be alright for Fliss and I to stay for a few days until we find somewhere to live. We've had a bit of a falling out with Lydia.'

'Ah.'

The Brigadier tightened the cord around his dressing gown so that it fitted snugly beneath his bulging stomach.

'That might be a bit of a problem,' he said, crossing his legs modestly. 'You see James, and this is not something that your mother and I planned for you or your brother Maurice to find out, but, you understand, since you were both at boarding school we had time on our hands to explore different avenues.' He lit a thick cigar and puffed hard before speaking further. 'The situation now is that your mother and I have become fervent swingers. *But*, we only swing on a Sunday. You see, we've been experiencing a few problems with the vicar ever since your mother's clamping episode at the church and I guess you could say that our activities have flourished into a replacement for Evening Worship. I do hope you'll understand.'

'Of course, of course,' said James, turning pale at the thought.

'And not a word to your mother,' the Brigadier added. 'Actually, I don't think she knows you're here. She's busy upstairs sorting out her smalls for this evening.'

James turned to Felicity who was busy trying to avert her eyes from a pair of leather handcuffs dangling from the Brigadier's dressing gown pocket. 'So, what do we do now?' he asked.

Felicity gripped her handbag. 'Let's try Mark,' she said, her stomach muscles tightening at the thought of Brigadier Peters getting aroused. 'Maybe we could crash there for a few nights.'

James gulped. 'Good idea,' he replied. 'Let's go now. I don't really want to be caught up in the stampede to my mother's boudoir.'

The Brigadier coughed disapprovingly. 'Now, now, James. Some respect, please. Your mother takes this event very seriously. She's had one of those Brazilian waxes especially for tonight. And I can tell you,' he added, lowering his voice in case his wife overheard, 'it's a damn sight cheaper than a new hairdo.'

James narrowed his eyes as he wondered what on earth his father was referring to. It sounded pretty explicit, all that reference to wax, he thought and glanced nervously over at the shiny, polished sideboard.

Felicity, meanwhile, on hearing Mrs Peters advance softly down the stairs in her fluffy pink slippers, grabbed James' hand and smartly led him out of the door. They leapt into the car and, after a few frenzied telephone calls, ended up sleeping on Mark's living room floor, glad that they had avoided some terrible event. As they lay beneath their beige duvet, they shivered when they considered what frolicking they might have encountered had they turned up at James' parents' home an hour later.

JOHN

On the 4th April, Felicity began her work as an assistant
solicitor at Meade, Pullen and Co Solicitors. She was shown
into a square room next to Marina's and immediately set to
work, trawling through the files that had lain untouched
by the loving hand of a lawyer for many a day. Felicity was
shocked by the spurious claims made by her new clients.
Did anyone really care if someone had been attacked by a
cat or tripped over a piece of linoleum? Obviously, yes. It
was bewildering. More importantly though, "no win, no
fee, agreements" meant that she was unlikely to make any
money at all from the dross that sat on her desk. There was
no way that she could reach her costs' target if she had to
rely on the ridiculous accusations made by angry pedestrians
and, worse still, there were numerous cases passed to her
from John where accidents had happened many years earlier
and proceedings had not been issued. Statute required that
the claims were brought to the court within three years. If
not, the firm would be sued as a result.

Felicity simply had no idea where to begin and half an
hour had passed in frustration before her portly secretary
entered and introduced herself.

'Hi, moy name's Jessica,' she informed Felicity in an almost incoherent cockney accent. 'Oi sit over there, opposite Mandy there with the grey hair.' She pointed to another large typist through the open door who waved at her with a thick wrist decorated with jangling bracelets. 'Just wundrin' if you'd loik a cuppa tea?'

'Any chance of a coffee?' asked Felicity. 'Milk, no sugar.'

'We only 'ave tea 'ere. You'll 'ave to bring in your own coffee granules if you want any of that fancy stuff.'

'Oh, right,' said Felicity, not wishing to rock the boat on her first day. 'In that case, tea will be fine.'

Jessica pinched her thin lips together. 'Oi'll sort out a mug for you, just for t'day. You'll need to bring in your own tomorra. The partners should 'ave told you the form 'ere before you started, you know.' Jessica turned and stomped off to the kitchenette.

Felicity looked out of the window onto the high street below. It was strangely quiet in her room, she thought, without the humming of a computer that, she assumed, would be installed later. In fact, she found the silence rather pleasant, even soothing. Gradually, though, the absence of noise heightened her appreciation of the soporific pinging noise ringing out from the secretaries' machines. Her eyes widened in horror as it slowly dawned on her that there were no computers at Meade Pullen. In fact, thinking back, all communications with the firm had been oral; there had been only a succession of abstract telephone calls, particularly with Dominic or bizarre conversations with Roger confirming her appointment. Before that first day, she had not seen their headed notepaper splodged with the secretaries' inky attempts at letter formation. Now she noticed that crucial bottles of correction fluid were perched next to the Royal Typewriters. She should have known better, Felicity realised, than to think that this firm could be anything but a disturbing place to work.

At lunchtime, Marina took Felicity out to lunch at the local pub to introduce her to some of the other members of staff. John Forrester was already leaning against the bar, fizzy lemonade in hand, when Felicity arrived. He looked Felicity up and down not in any sexual way, but merely to assess whether or not his suspicious wife would approve of her in the firm. He noted her well-cut suit, her over-high heels and her dark hair swept up into a ponytail and breathed a sigh of relief; Felicity was far too skinny to have any effect on his flabby libido. She even appeared to be wearing a bra that was several sizes too large, her non-existent breasts cowering beneath the lacy material.

'So,' he said, without bothering to introduce himself, 'you were a chalet girl, weren't you?'

'Sorry? A chalet girl? I don't think so,' replied Felicity somewhat surprised at this man's less than charming approach.

'Yes you were. I saw your CV.'

'I think you're mistaken.' Felicity looked blankly at her inquisitor noting, with some disdain, that he wore a curry stained tie and old, worn shoes. A few spiralling chest hairs protruded through a space in his shirt where a button should have been and, oddly, his accent constantly veered from upper middle class to cockney and then back again. Who on earth was this man?

'I'm quite sure you've confused me with someone else,' she replied. It was indeed true that Felicity was a competent skier but she had never taken a paid holiday in her life.

Felicity smiled politely and swivelled around to face Marina whose head was already immersed in her second bag of pork scratchings.

'So,' the grubby man said as he reappeared at her side and persisted in dominating her attention. 'Are you any good at making money?' Felicity took a sip from the glass of sparkling water that Marina had kindly bought her, shifting her weight away from the annoying little urchin who was still tweaking her elbow.

'If you're talking about costs,' she replied, not bothering to hide her irritation, 'and I assume that you are, then you'll have to wait and see. Quite frankly, wouldn't it be more sensible to ask me in six months' time?'

John grinned, the corners of his lips disappearing into his thick cheeks. 'Well, you may say that now, but I think it's important for you to realise that costs are what it's all about at Meade Pullen. Nothing more, nothing less.' John shrugged his sloping shoulders, annoyed that he had failed to capture Felicity's full attention. 'I'm just trying to help,' he mumbled, stepping even closer. Felicity leaned away from him, hoping that the monologue might end there but it didn't. 'Our best legal executive is Dave Vallely.' John pointed to a tall, willowy man glowering at her from a dark corner. 'He bills over 200K every year and that's the figure you'll have to beat if you want to get anywhere here.'

'Well, thanks for the advice.' Felicity placed her glass on the bar. 'If what you say is right, I'd better be getting back to the office. See you.'

Mid afternoon, Jessica presented Felicity with the six letters that she had typed that day. As Felicity read through them she was appalled to see the number of basic errors. White correction fluid blessed almost every line and she had no alternative other than to tear them up and chuck them in the bin.

Over the next three weeks, the typing situation did not improve and Felicity felt that she had to speak to one of the partners about it. She considered the odd selection of lawyers who fulfilled that criterion. Roger had his head permanently in the clouds; Maximilian Hornet, the managing partner was only interested in his employees' breast size and was therefore immediately disappointed by Felicity's arrival; and Tarquin and Lucian were hardly ever in the office. Marina occupied the room next to her but always kept her door firmly shut and was therefore oblivious to the chaotic secretarial situation that existed within feet from her desk.

'I can't go on with Jessica working for me,' Felicity complained as she walked into Marina's room. 'Nothing is getting done. You're paying me to get some results and I'm not achieving anything. If these claims are to be turned around quickly, I must have secretarial support to do so. Otherwise, I might as well not bother.'

Marina drummed her scarily small hands on her desk. Felicity's salary was a sore subject for Marina who had been furious when she realised the size of it.

'I understand your concerns, Felicity, but it's just that, as you may have noticed, we're quite old school here. We like claims to roll along merrily until someone, preferably the Defendant, puts forward an offer. Best not to get too pushy. That's what I would advise.'

Felicity gasped. 'But this is supposed to be a litigation firm! Don't the clients ever ask why their cases aren't being prepared for trial or taking so long to settle?'

'No, not really. If a client is a being a bit tricky, we simply tell them that their claims are being dealt with in the same way as everyone else's. And it's true. That way it's difficult for them to complain. It's simple really.'

'But that's outrageous.'

'No, not at all. It works for us here at Meade Pullen,' Marina explained curtly. Felicity tried another tack.

'I'm really sorry, Marina,' she said, 'but I simply cannot continue to work with Jessica. She's been leaving me out of the carrot cake round. I see her wafting by with the patisserie trolley, day in, day out and she has never once asked me if I'd fancy a slice. I consider that to be extremely rude and highly discourteous to me. Possibly it's *discrimination*.'

Marina sat up straight. 'Well, that's a different matter altogether,' she replied curtly. 'We strive to be one great big happy family here.' Marina paused to hand Felicity a fresh cream éclair. 'Actually, I thought I heard a bit of argy-bargy over the custard slices just the other day. Clearly that's not on. Leave it with me. I'll sort her out.'

*

From that day on, Felicity pumped up the pressure on Jessica. She doubled her amount of dictation each day and criticised Jessica for each and every typographical error. It took only five days of icy silence until Jessica handed in her notice.

'Oi just wanted to let you know, Felicity,' she barked, 'that you won't get nowhere in this firm if you push too hard. No one else has ever been asked to re-type a letter and if you keep on doing that, you won't be very popular with the next person who has the misfortune to work for you. Good riddance.' Jessica picked up her orange mug and marched out of the building.

A slow smile spread over Felicity's face. She had won. It had been agreed that Jessica's replacement would be Marina's secretary, the only young enthusiastic secretary in the firm - Valerie Napier.

*

Over the next few, blissful weeks with Valerie, Felicity continued to bring all her cases up to speed: she settled over ten and issued proceedings in the local County Court on eight others. Matters were progressing and she felt proud of her work as her caseload began to take shape. Even the clients occasionally showed their gratitude, thankful that their claims were no longer lying silent. Best of all, she was beginning to make some money.

Felicity had hardly seen Roger during this time and, fully aware that it would do her career nothing but good to keep in close contact with him, she decided to pay him a visit.

'So, Miss Garrett. *Felicity*,' Roger said, unintentionally leering at the young solicitor as she walked into his office. 'How are you getting on?'

Felicity fluttered her eyelashes. 'Fine, I think,' she replied. 'Anyway, you're the best judge of that.' She ran a dainty hand over her neat backside as a reminder and watched Roger crumble. 'But I think I could do with some more work, though, and I was wondering if I might unburden your load by taking over the clinical negligence files? That's all I really specialised in at my previous firm.'

'Yes, I remember now. What an excellent idea! I'll get my secretary to bring some over straight away. Actually,' he said quietly, loosening his tie, 'I've got rather a lot on at the moment,' he added, referring to the expansion of his trout farm and not to any legal dilemma.

Felicity smiled. 'It will suit us both then. I'll look forward to going through them.' She turned to walk away but Roger, concerned that she was about to leave his presence, twittered on desperately.

'So,' he blurted, a little too impetuously, 'are you dating anyone at the moment?' Roger was horrified at the ease with which his mouth had uttered such painfully inappropriate words and in confusion he began shuffling the paper on his desk. 'I mean, I mean, everything else alright? No problems with dates, I mean court dates, obviously,' he added, pulling himself together. Damn those ankles, he thought. They were leading him astray.

'Yes, fine thanks.' Felicity congratulated herself. This meeting was turning out just as she had planned. 'Valerie has recently become my secretary,' she explained, 'so things are looking up.'

'Excellent news! So you're not going to leave us quite yet?'

'No, you needn't worry about that.'

'Good.' Roger's shoulders relaxed. 'By the way, don't let Valerie's antics bother you.'

Felicity looked confused. 'Sorry?' she asked. 'What do you mean?'

'She's a very popular girl with the male legal executives, if you get my gist.'

'Ah, I see,' replied Felicity, nodding slowly. 'Well, what she does in her spare time is up to her.'

'That's the problem; it's not always in her spare time, so just beware.' Roger could feel himself getting hot and bothered as the ankles that he so admired rotated enticingly before him as their owner backed out of his room. 'Good luck,' he added, beads of sweat accumulating beneath his thick hair.

As soon as the door had closed shut, Roger swung round and round in his rotating chair to cool his heated brow and had only just come to a standstill when he felt vibration in the top left hand drawer of his antique desk. He quickly pulled out the gold plated telephone and lifted the receiver.

'Baron?'

'Hiya, Rog. You don't mind me calling you Rog, do you?' Roger's fingers clenched. It was the voice from the valleys.

'Not at all, Baron,' he replied. 'And what can I do for you this fine day?' Roger was hopeful that the conversation with the Baron would not be a precursor to yet another trout delivery. Weeks had passed since he last botched up a claim and another cruise with Pamela had meant that he hadn't been able to fish as often as he would have liked.

'I just want you to look up out of your window for a minute.'

Roger spun round to see the Baron's helicopter swaying above King's Cross Station and an orange/brown face leaning out precariously into space. He waved and watched his benefactor wave back. 'And what brings you to these parts, Baron?' he asked.

'Well, two reasons, actually, Rog.'

'Yes?'

'Firstly, I've been thinking long and hard about diversifying my inventions. I've spent many a long hour when the Baroness has been swimming, perfecting her strokes - there's an important gala coming up - creating a cheaper pole for the less well-off camper. It's made of hotdogs rather than prime meat sausages, and is therefore far more affordable.'

'What a marvellous idea.'

'Why, thank you. I think so too. That's why I'm yur in London to visit the Queen.'

'Sorry?'

'No, not really, Rog. I just like saying that. To be truthful, I've an appointment with an 'ot-dog skin man in Hackney in 'alf an hour and I thought I'd call in on you on the off chance since I was passing, like.'

'And I'm pleased that you thought of me.'

'Yes, well, as you know, Rog, Meade Pullen is never really very far from the forefront of this great mind of mine,' he said, tapping his head reassuringly. 'In fact, it's one of

Meade Pullen's partners that brings me onto my second reason for flying above this wondrous city.' The Baron paused as a screaming noise followed by intense scrabbling briefly interrupted the conversation. 'Sorry, Roger, where was I?' he continued.

'Not sure, Baron.' Roger scanned the horizon desperately; anxious that nothing untoward had happened to the firm's "bank". 'Is everything alright up there?'

'Nothin' wrong, Rog. No, nothin' wrong up yer.'

Roger, unconvinced, reached for his glasses and could just about make out a strange black hairy object floating through the sky. He peered at it more carefully, his eyes widening in horror as he realised that the falling mass of hair closely resembled the Baron's wig.

'Oh, yes, now I remember what I wanted to ask you.'

Roger coughed loudly by way of response, too traumatised by the wig incident to speak whilst the Baron continued, unperturbed. 'I just wanted to check on how my little sister is doing. All right is she? It's just that she's been behavin' a bit strange as of late and I want to make sure that nothin' has upset her. She hasn't found out about our trout deal, I 'ope?'

Roger emitted a frightening wheezing noise that originated from somewhere deep within before speaking. 'No, I wouldn't have thought so,' he said. 'Marina is fine.'

'Good God alive! Don't tell me she's still calling herself that silly name! My mam would turn in her little grave if she knew that her Mari had discarded her Celtic heritage!'

Roger cleared his throat. 'Maybe you could talk to her about it?'

'Well, to be honest with you, Rog, I don't think that will be possible for a while. Mari and I have had a minor falling-out over some sausages she guzzled last time she was stayin'.' The Baron shook his naked head. 'She can't stop herself sometimes. And, what was worse was that she doused them in the Baroness' specially brewed cod liver oil, as well. There was trouble abounding at Ty Bach, I can tell you.'

'I'm sure.'

'Anyway, must dash. My pilot has just booked me in for an urgent hair appointment so I'll have to fly.' The Baron laughed at his joke. 'I love saying that, too.'

*

Felicity had been left slightly puzzled by Roger's remarks concerning her secretary and these concerns were heightened when, on her way back to her office, she caught a fleeting glimpse of Valerie in Dave Vallely's room. Whilst standing near the water cooler to grab a glass of water, she could just about make out Dave's low voice interspersed with Valerie's high-pitched giggles.

Felicity returned to her room and waited. Twenty minutes passed until her secretary finally reappeared, looking flustered and slightly pink in the cheek.

'Everything all right?' she asked Felicity, patting down her ruffled hair.

'Absolutely, thanks Valerie. I was just wondering where you had been, that's all. I need you to do some urgent work for me. The tape's on top of the files over there.' Felicity pointed to a stack of cardboard files piled up on the floor in front of her desk. 'By the way, weren't you about to tell me what you had been doing?'

Valerie straightened up, beadily eyeing Felicity. 'I've been busy photocopying those medical records on that Gerrard case for you. You said you wanted the papers to go out to Counsel tonight.'

'So I did.' Felicity scrutinised her secretary's pointed face. Pretty, she thought, but in an *obvious* sort of way.

'Is there a photocopying machine in Mr Vallely's room, Valerie? Because, you see, I suspect, although I cannot be certain, that I saw in you in there and I suspect, although again, I cannot be certain, that you were in there for some time.'

'If you must know,' Valerie bristled. 'I was in there for a few minutes discussing a private matter.'

'Really?' said Felicity, raising her neat eyebrows. 'Oh well, in that case, that's fine. Let's get on then, shall we? I need to finish some bills so, if you don't mind, why don't you get back to your desk? You've plenty to be getting on with. And you can take those statute barred files back to John. He can sort out his own mess, not me.' Felicity picked up her calculator and waited impatiently for her secretary to heave the files out of the room before writing a '£' sign at the top of her notepad.

*

Two weeks later, Sarah Kelleher became the latest recruit to Meade, Pullen and Co. John Forrester went to greet her in reception.

'Hi, Sarah. Good to see you again,' he said, grimacing awkwardly and scratching his head. Rather than grasping her outstretched hand, he left it to dangle in mid-air, disliking any form of physical contact with anyone, even his malevolent wife.

'Good to see you too.'

'Right. Come with me. Your office is next to mine. It's a bit on the small size but it'll do for the moment.' John turned and strode off, leading Sarah through a maze of corridors until he reached two doors situated at right angles to one another. He opened the one in front of him to reveal a tiny box room and allowed Sarah to enter first before following her in so that the two of them stood shoulder to shoulder in front of the child-sized desk. This close proximity was a big mistake for John who was now having his unusually large area of personal space invaded. He began to perspire heavily, seething that he was not wearing his suit jacket.

'Everything alright?' Sarah asked, aware that her work colleague had become somewhat distressed.

'I'll be back in a moment,' he replied, hopping from one foot to the other. 'I need to check the post.'

John disappeared into his office and closed the door. He picked up his much-needed jacket and headed straight for the men's lavatories. He preferred reading through the day's letters in there; he would not be disturbed and would not have to worry about the dark circles expanding around his armpits. With the folds of his trousers encasing his ankles he put the letters into his own order of importance. At the top of the pile he placed the threatening letters from his opponents together with the Orders from the court, next came the hostile letters from his clients seeking some (any) information on the status of their claims; and at the bottom of the heap were the demands for payment from medical experts. 'Don't pay them unless they squeal' was the order from the managing partner, who never wished to see a penny of bank interest lost. John, being the meddlesome soul that he was, would also "check" other people's post whilst in his cubicle, under the pretence of Regulatory requirements. This requirement was, indeed, a valid one but was generally delegated to one of the partners rather than a prying assistant who only had his own interest at heart.

Finally, John checked to see whether there were any letters from defendant solicitors keen to point out that his own clients' claims had failed. He had already passed all his dud files to Felicity and scribbled her initials on every letter that came in relating to those cases. By checking the post every morning, he could make sure that none of the angrier correspondence ever landed on his own desk.

Having completed his daily function, John felt sufficiently calmed to be able to re-enter Sarah's room.

'I think I should explain that you're going to be assisting me with the noise induced hearing loss cases; it's low value, high turnover stuff and it'll be ideal for you to start with whilst you settle in.' He turned to leave. 'By the way, you'll have to be introduced to Felicity Garrett later on. She's the other new girl in the office next to Marina, the, er, rather large lady. I'd do it myself but, er.' The tips of John's ears began to turn crimson as he spotted one of his cast-off "dud" files sitting on Sarah's desk.

'Must dash.'

IN RESIDENCE

'James, my love, we really can't go on staying at your parents, *ad infinitum*.' Felicity carefully spread a thin layer of butter onto a triangle of toast as James peered at her over the top of his newspaper. He had been revelling in the layout of *The Telegraph* business section, an unusual treat for him. Felicity liked to take *The Times* but now he was at home he could indulge in his family's favourite broadsheet. After all, as his father had said, *The Times* was no better than reading a tabloid in its present, piddlingly tiny form.

'What was that you said, my darling?' James asked vaguely, momentarily distracted by a Close Encounters Ad. He encircled it in red ink before glancing up at Felicity's earnest face.

'I think that we should start focussing a bit more on finding a place to live, don't you?'

'Mmm. Maybe,' James replied, a tad *distrait*, Felicity thought.

In fact, James was really rather enjoying being back at home; he hadn't spent much time there during his youth and felt that he was now making up for it. His parents had reluctantly agreed to the pair staying despite their Sunday night antics as Mark's flat was clearly too cramped for them to stay long term. More importantly, when James formally quit his flat in Fulham, Lydia went completely berserk and spitefully released all her rodents into his bedroom. His bedclothes were in tatters.

James looked down again at the newspaper as Felicity sipped her Earl Grey tea. All that political stuff seemed to make more sense to him now, he thought. He was even getting to grips with the term *referendum* and was really enjoying the sparkling conversations with his father after dinner over a glass of the finest malt (or two, if Mummy had retired to bed) in which they debated, in particular, as to whether the plural for referendum was referendums or referenda. It was all very stimulating. He also liked the way that his mother's cleaning lady ironed for him and the fact that he could travel to work safe in the knowledge that his shirts were not decorated with scorch marks as they often were when Felicity tampered with them.

Felicity persisted with her line of thought. 'I really don't think that I can manage to sit through another Sunday night's *sermon*, shall we call it?' she said. 'Hearing your father giggle like that is really quite unnatural.'

James put down his paper onto the table. 'Oh, it isn't that bad. You can always turn up the volume on the telly.'

'No, James. I'm serious. We need to have a place of our own. Remember how we dreamed of decorating our flat? Floral prints? Chintz covered cushions? It was to have been our own little cottage in the city.' James looked confused. 'We've got no alternative, James. We'll have to buy.'

The cogs slowly started to turn but James still found it extremely difficult to retrieve the image of idyllic home life with Fliss. He wiggled his toes inside his father's slippers. Mmm, he thought as his toenails became entwined with the fluffy insides. That felt nice.

'James? Are you listening?'

'Yes, yes.'

James tried hard to sit up straight but the ends of his dressing gown had become lodged under the leg of the chair forcing him into a curious curled position. He struggled to unravel himself.

'What on earth are you doing now? Sit up.'

James lifted up the chair leg and did as he was told. 'Tell you what, Fliss. I'll speak to that old school chum of mine. Eddie something Jones is his name. He's a bigwig in that estate agency on the High Street - his father owns it I think - and I'll ask him to keep his ear to the ground for a little bargain for us. Shouldn't take too long.' James picked up the newspaper again. 'What was that word you said earlier? Ad fini?'

'Ad infinitum?'

'Yes, that's it. So what does it mean, then?'

Felicity, having spent a tedious half hour removing mould from all the preserves, spread a dollop of thinly cut marmalade onto another piece of toast cutting it into six identically sized squares.

'Forever, James. Forever,' she explained slowly, handing him the plate.

'Thanks,' he said, nodding, and repeated the "new" phrase quietly under his coffee-smelling breath. 'I might use it at work today.' He folded up the paper. 'You know, Fliss,' he said, excitedly, 'since we've been staying here my mind has become like a dictionary, maybe even a wotsit, a thesaurus. I'm a wild, questioning beast of a man. I'm sure it's my parents' influence bringing out the best in me, you know.'

Felicity took a sharp intake of breath. 'That's usually what childhood achieves, James, not when you're ambling towards middle age.' She dabbed at her mouth with a

Damask napkin. 'I'll be late for work if I don't get a move on.'

Felicity walked over to the bottom of the Peters' oak staircase and turned, delicately placing her manicured hand on the banisters. 'Don't forget to call Eddie the Estate agent will you?' James nodded, his mouth brimming with crumbs. 'And another thing, James, I really don't think I can bear any longer to hear your mother bleating on about how beautiful she thinks she once was. She's been dumpy and plain ever since she was a toddler and it's about time she faced facts. If we're still here in six weeks time, I'm afraid that I might have to put her straight.'

'Of course not. I'll call him right away.' James wiped a dribble of butter from his chin and gazed sadly at one of the black and white stills of his mother whose sausage-like legs were oozing out of a pair of jodhpurs. 'Sorry,' he whispered to the photograph, realising that Felicity's harsh words were, in fact, quite true.

*

Only two days later, Felicity and James began their quest by tramping around West London viewing numerous dingy properties with Eddie. None came close to being suitable, but, just as they were beginning to give up hope, Felicity spotted the details of a flat on Ladbroke Grove in windows of another, less flashy, estate agency. She went to see it alone without waiting for James to lumber in all sweaty and enthusiastic this being the worst thing, in her view, for a vendor to see. Felicity considered the flat to be the closest property to fit the bill that she had seen and so she put in an offer well below the asking price. Negotiations then ensued with another over enthusiastic estate agent named Phil.

'Hi, Felicity, my love,' said Phil when he called to deliver the news that her offer had been rejected. 'Bad news, I'm afraid, your offer's too low. It's been rejected.'

'Oh.'

It was a big mistake to a) call her "Felicity" when she clearly left a message stating that "Miss Garrett" had called, and b) have the nerve to call her "my love" when there was certainly no possibility of Felicity ever having an estate agent as "her love".

'I've tried telling them that your offer is a realistic one but, you know, Felicity?' Felicity seethed. 'They're stubborn people, these vendors. But, between you and me, and I know that I shouldn't be saying this to you, since they are my clients and so on, but I think they're asking a bit too much for that flat. Tell you what, you put the offer up a bit by, let's say, another two grand and I'll see what I can do for you. How does that grab you?'

'To be perfectly honest with you, I take the view that my offer was entirely reasonable. The kitchen's the size of a shoe box and there's not even an oven.'

'But, Felicity, darling, listen.'

He must surely be gay if he thinks he can get away with such familiarities, thought Felicity.

'You'll be eating out every night so there'll be no need for an oven! That's why you're moving to fashionable Notting Hill - to enjoy the numerous bars and restaurants!'

'Actually, it's Ladbroke Grove.'

'Come, come. It's all the same these days.'

Felicity rolled her eyes. 'I'll up it by a thousand pounds and that's my final offer.' She put the phone down not wishing to prolong the conversation with Philip any longer.

Half an hour later he rang to confirm that the flat was hers.

To save money after failing to budget purchasing costs, Felicity decided to undertake the arduous task of her own conveyancing. Since she had never excelled at land law this was potentially something of a problem and, even months later, there was a strong possibility that they should be living next door.

VALERIE

On the day that Sarah joined Meade, Pullen and Co, Valerie and Dave spent the evening in *The Bull* Public House. They snuggled up close to one another in their favourite dark corner; their heads only inches apart, desperately hoping that none of their work colleagues would join them.

'Wot time are you expected back tonite then, my lickle treasure?' Dave asked.

Valerie giggled and flicked her blonde, highlighted hair over her shoulder. 'Depends how long you want me,' she teased. 'Ray's gone owt bowlin' wiv 'is mates, so it could be any time, really.'

'Fancy anover, then?'

'Ooh, not arf.' Valerie took a swig from her glass, wiped the excess from her mouth with the back of her hand and belched. ''Scuse, me!' she giggled.

'You're a right one, you are!' chuckled Dave, his shoulders jerking up and down with the force of his hilarity. 'You're bleeding mad. That's wot you are! Ho, ho,' he teased, squeezing Valerie's knee.

Dave walked over to the bar, still chortling to himself and soon returned with a couple of double vodkas. After sliding his bottom back into his still-warm seat, he placed a firm hand on Valerie's right thigh. 'You 'av no idea 'ow much you turn me on, you lickle devil.'

'Stop that, Dave. I'm nearly a married woman!'

'Ain't made no difference so far!'

'Anyway,' Valerie continued after removing the errant hand, 'wot I want to know from you, young man, is what you fink of fancy Felicity?'

'Well,' he replied, after some deliberation, 'there's some who might say she's attractive. But not me. I ain't into that ice-maiden fing.'

'I don't mean wevver you fancy her, yer little tinker. Wot I mean is wot you fink of her getting the costs in.' Valerie slurped at her vodka, having removed a limp slice of lemon with her fingers and slopped it into the ashtray. 'Ya know, Dave, I reckon she's overtaken you already.'

'Wot?'

'Yeah! You'd better realise you've got some serious competition wiv that gurl.'

'I see.'

Dave's gnome-like features were beginning to turn puce with rage. He gripped his glass so tightly that the insides of his fingers turned completely white.

'You awright, Dave? You look a bit angry.' There was no reply. Valerie chirruped on. 'It's only a few cheques that go into the partners' pockets anyhow. That's wot we're torkin' abat 'ere; nuffink serious, ya know?'

After a few more minutes' silence, Dave was finally able to speak through clenched teeth.

'You don't understand, do you Val? It's all abat targets. If that gurl starts beating me, the partners will put my target sky 'igh an' all, and that'll mean less wonger for me each year. Don't you see? This is serious stuff. I do not, under any circumstance want to be knocked off the numba one position in the firm. It'll be no more lickle nights owt for you an' me if I don't get me bonus.'

Valerie bit her nails anxiously and, much as she tried, was unable to stop herself looking glum, well aware that it did nothing for her jowls. Dave, however, was oblivious to any of her facial indiscretions and harped on, regardless.

'In all my fifteen years at Meade Pullen, no one, not no one has ever come close to making my level of costs and oi do not intend letting that posh little cow get the better of me now. I'll see to that, you mark moy words.'

'Awright, awright. Calm down Dave. Don't get riled over that Felicity. You'll always be number one in my eyes.' Valerie batted her eyelashes, thick with blue mascara. 'We're 'aving a luverly drinky poo out togevver. Come on. Drink up. Let's celebrate.'

'Celebrate wot?'

'Oh, I dunno. There's gotta be sumfing. 'Ow about you and me just being owt togevver, alone? Isn't that enuff?'

'I know, I know, but I just can' 'elp it. That target stuff makes me livid.' Dave jutted his neck forward and loosened his Burberry tie, trying to calm himself. 'Tell you wot,' he said after a while, staring optimistically at her cleavage. 'I reckon a lickle more flesh might do the trick.' He licked his thick lips in anticipation.

'Ooh, you are a one!' Valerie, always keen to oblige, slowly unbuttoned the top of her blouse to reveal two round cannons ready to pop. She pulled back her shoulders dramatically, preparing for adulation. Dave, taking his cue, ceremoniously viewed the explosives. 'Ya know, I feel better already!' he said, taking Valerie's hand and kissing it passionately. 'Fank you, sweet angel.'

*

The following day, Felicity was sitting at her desk when the telephone rang. She picked up the receiver; it was Marina calling from her room next door.

'I was wondering if you'd be willing to come to a supervisors' meeting this afternoon? The partners thought you might like to become more involved in the running of the firm, albeit at a very minor level, and also with supervision of the staff. Would that suit you?' Felicity could hear Marina's voice echoing through the thin partition wall.

'And whom do you propose that I supervise?' she asked.

'Just two or three fee earners, probably only Gareth and John. We're hoping to gain an Investors In People award in a few years' time and we need to have some form of cascading management system in place. You wouldn't have to do much, just check through a few files now and again and fill in some forms. That's all. It would be quite simple.'

Felicity sat back in her chair. A supervisory role in only three months of being at the firm! Well, she thought smugly, that hadn't taken long to achieve! Not bad for someone who hadn't even started playing the partnership game yet.

At the allotted hour, Felicity strolled into Marina's room. The Baroness, recently ensconced in the position of Practice Manager was already taking up much of the small room since, as ever, she refused to wear anything but her various flowing pastel evening gowns made of the finest chiffon. Gareth Roberts and Dave Vallely were already seated and Felicity had to cram herself against one of the cabinets as Marina opened the meeting.

'Right, first things first,' she said, eyeing the Baroness suspiciously. 'Let's sort out who supervises whom.' Marina turned towards Dave, her breasts bouncing wildly against one another as if competing for position, 'I think you should supervise Delyth and Ffion since they're on the same floor as you; Felicity, you can supervise Gareth and John; and Gareth, let's see.' Marina's dancing boobs came to a grinding halt as she squeezed her elbows flat against her sides. 'You can have Sarah and Dave. I'll have Roger, who, I can assure you, will be a total nightmare, and Peter.' Marina looked at the potential cluster of supervisors seated before her. 'Have I missed anyone out?'

'What about Felicity?'

'Oh, yes. Well how about you doing it, Dave? Felicity's pretty organised so it shouldn't be too much of a problem.'

'Yeah, that's fine by me.' Dave grinned. 'I was going to suggest it, actually.'

'Good. Have you managed to minute everything, Baroness?'

'Yes, it's all here in short hand,' she replied, twirling her pencil around the two fingers of one hand to demonstrate her secretarial skills.

'So only you can understand it?'

'Of course.'

Marina glanced at her small silver wristwatch, embedded into her flesh like a silicon chip, and continued with the meeting. Felicity listened to her colleagues drone on endlessly about the firm's tittle-tattle, realising that it was hardly the high-powered breakfast assignation that she had envisaged as she completed her application form for a place on the Legal Practice Course. Where were all the frivolous champagne parties that she had promised herself? Drifting smartly down the Thames by the looks of things.

'Right then folks,' Marina said, obviously aroused. She had waited for this moment for some time, possibly twelve months. 'We need to sort out plans for the Christmas party. My view is that we should branch out from the sherry and mince pies we've had for the past few years. How about something more, more,' she searched for the precise word, 'more contemporary?'

All eyes widened.

'And, er, so, what do you mean?' asked Gareth, normally mute but sufficiently worried by this random suggestion to voice his concerns.

'I think that following the appointment of Felicity and Sarah and the injection of new female blood and so on, we should be demonstrating to the staff that we have progressed from nibbles in the Boardroom. I suggest we take on the twenty first century with aplomb.' Beads of excitement splattered Marina's forehead. 'We need to spice up the festivities! Let's have streamers; let's have balloons! Let's have Kiss-Me-Quick hats!' Marina's arms flailed, untamed and wobbly, over her desk causing papers to fly hither and thither.

'Let's have an Ann Summers' party!' The Baroness piped up, caught up in the thrill of the moment.

Marina bit her hairy upper lip. 'That was not quite what I had in mind. Maybe next year. But thank you, Baroness, for your proposal.'

'How about a black-tie do at The Grosvenor?' Felicity volunteered, feeling more at home with the subject of party venues than supervision. 'We had a splendid evening there last year when I was at Roberts Blackman. The firm paid for us all to stay in the hotel for the night. It was absolutely marvellous fun.'

'I don't think that it's really Meade Pullen's sort of thing,' explained Marina. 'We want something that everyone is going to be comfortable with. The trouble, Felicity, is that half the staff wouldn't know how to eat a meal without ketchup let alone use a serviette.'

'You mean a napkin.'

'Whatever. Just think of somewhere else.'

All were silent for a few embarrassing seconds until Dave piped up. 'How about *The Blushing Widow*?'

'Now that's a good idea, Dave. Could you find out how much it would cost etc?'

'Yeah, no problemo. I'll drop in on me way 'ome.'

There being no further business, the meeting was closed.

*

Dave telephoned Valerie as soon as he was safely seated at his desk.

'Hiya Gorgeous! Fancy a break from the old bag's bills?'

'Hello? Who is this?' giggled Valerie, distractedly winding the telephone cord around her forefinger.

'Who do ya fink it is?' teased Dave. 'I can tell you somefink for nuffin', there ain't many people who would call *you* gorgeous!'

'Very funny, Dave. I'll come down in a minute. I just need to make sure that Felicity don't see me go.'

'Tell you wot. Meet me by the stockroom. I'll fetch the key.'

Valerie replaced the receiver and finished off the bill she had been preparing. She popped her head round the door to Felicity's office and said that she was just nipping downstairs to copy some invoices.

Felicity, heavily engrossed in a file, made no response.

Valerie's white heels clicked down the stone steps as she made her way to the basement. The stockroom door had been unlocked and was slightly ajar. Valerie gingerly pulled it wide open to allow a streak of light from the stairwell into the pitch-black dungeon of a room. Row upon row of old files were revealed, carefully stacked high on dusty shelves where they waited their turn, in years to come, for their final destruction.

'Hello? Anybody there?' Valerie giggled nervously. Dave swaggered out from the shadows and grabbed her from behind. He put both his arms around her ample waist and pulled her towards him. 'Mmm. You smell bootiful,' he said, nuzzling her neck. 'Come over 'ere. I've got somefink to show ya.' He took Valerie's hand and led her to the back of the stockroom. 'Look!' he whispered as he handed her a rectangular box. 'I've bought you a present.'

'Wot on earth is this?'

Dave laughed loudly. 'Wot do ya fink it is, ya daft bird?' Dave replied pinching her midriff. 'It's a vibrator! I bought it wiv me bonus. The woman in the shop said it was a best seller. Look 'ere. I'll show ya 'ow it works.'

Dave retrieved the vibrator from Valerie's cold hands and, trembling with anticipation, yanked at the switch. Quick as a flash, the machine was off! It rotated and shook like an angry vicar's finger wagging at an insolent boy. On high speed, it might have been handy to loosen brickwork.

'Hold on tight, Valerie. This baby's ready for action!' Dave exclaimed in his best American accent, carefully cultivated to woo the ladies. He pulled at Valerie's tight skirt, attempting to lift it. 'Jesus, Val, wot you been eating?' he exclaimed, forgetting his intentions to charm. 'This fing's stuck tight.'

Valerie huffed loudly. 'Let me do it.' She pulled the skirt back down to its usual mid-thigh length as Dave worked wonders with his fly, deftly whipping off his slinky, black y-fronts.

'Ooh, I want you, Babe,' his said, returning to his Elvis impersonation (he was a life-long fan and knew each and every line of the King's movies-even the Hawaiian ones). 'You drive me crazy, kid.'

Dave pulled Valerie towards him with his free non-vibrating hand and began nibbling at the skin on her neck. He had seen Elvis do this nibbling bit to a "broad" and hoped that it would have the same knee weakening effect on Valerie. He bared his gnashers, ready for action, and lunged forward at full speed at an ill-prepared Valerie.

Suddenly, they heard a voice shout out from the other side of the stockroom door. 'Who's in there? What's going on?' it asked. The doorknob rattled, striking fear into the courting couple's hearts.

'You locked the door didn't you?' Valerie asked, tugging desperately at her skirt.

''Course I did. Wot do ya take me for?'

'Anyone in there?' came the voice again.

Dave, pulling on his pants with rather less flourish than was executed during their removal, dropped the gyrating vibrator onto the concrete floor and watched in amazement as it proceeded to advance, crab-like, in a north, north-easterly direction until it finally found a suitable resting place in the file of Dickens v Tolson 1987.

'What the fuck do we do now?' spat Valerie in the tone normally reserved for the most tiresome of clients.

'Well, I certainly ain't doing nuffing until this geezer has settled down.' Dave looked angrily at his offending appendage. 'We'll just 'ave to sit it out.'

Twenty minutes later, Valerie was seated at her desk, makeup only marginally awry.

'I've been searching for you,' said Felicity, marching towards her secretary's desk.

'Really? I've been doing that photocopying you wanted.'

'Where?'

'On the second floor.'

'I looked for you there.'

'I had to spend quite some time in the loo as well. Time of the month, you know,' Valerie whispered, hoping that some female complaint might engender sympathy.

'Whatever,' Felicity snapped dismissively. 'I'm going to a conference with Counsel this afternoon and I've run out of notepads. I'll have to nip down to the stockroom to fetch a new one.'

'I'll get it,' volunteered Valerie, jumping out of her chair.

'No, it's all right, thanks. I heard some strange noises down there earlier so I might have a look to see what was going on. You stay right where you are.' Felicity walked towards the stairs. 'In your condition it's probably best that you remain seated, anyway.'

Valerie looked straight ahead, desperate not to catch a glance from any of the other secretaries and pretended to type a letter. As soon as she was certain that Felicity was safely out of earshot she rang Dave.

'Hi, it's me,' she said, urgently.

'Hi, Babe.'

'You've got the, er, *new toy*, 'aven't you?' Valerie's voice quivered as she spoke.

'No, Darlin'. I 'aven't 'ad time. John's been in 'ere sniffing arand an' I 'aven't 'ad a chance to nip dan.'

'Oh, shit.'

'Wot's wrong, Babe?'

'Felicity's down there now. It was 'er who was outside the door earlier on.'

'Oh, shit.'

'Zactly.'

*

At 3pm that afternoon, Felicity had her first conference with Geoffrey Carter QC. Roger had asked her to take over the Connolly case as the trial dates coincided with the village Annual Trout Festival and Felicity, keen to ensure that no stone had been left unturned by Roger, had swiftly arranged the meeting with Counsel. It was common knowledge within the legal profession that the most troublesome claims were frequently left to fester until some new recruit appeared, all eager and fresh-faced. Files were then quickly dusted down and handed to their new master within a matter of days. Felicity was concerned that she might now be the unfortunate recipient of a doomed case in its last dying stages. She was right. Roger had failed to draft and serve a Schedule of Loss and was, consequently, so concerned that the case might be struck out at any moment, had already teed up the Baron to expect a large delivery of fish in return for a handful of his finest emeralds. Roger was, as always, grateful that the Baron didn't mind parting too much with his gems and also that the Baroness, fast approaching another birthday, had decided to treble her intake of Omega 3 oils.

Felicity marched into Geoffrey's lair, oblivious to the large mirror placed carefully behind the door to allow him to consider each and every aspect of his instructing solicitors. This is more like it, thought Geoffrey, catching a cheeky glimpse of Felicity's figure hugging skirt.

'Do sit down.'

Geoffrey drew out a chair for her. 'Let me take those heavy files from you.' He ran a thin, grey tongue over his plastic teeth.

'So,' he said, once he had seated himself opposite his new plaything, his blood pressure starting to rise. 'How are you getting on at Meade Pullen?'

Felicity blinked slowly at her interrogator before replying. She explained that she was always busy which, she thought, was a good thing.

'Absolutely,' agreed Geoffrey nodding sagely. 'They're a queer bunch though, aren't they?' He paused momentarily to leer. 'I'm sure you'll forgive me if you think I'm stepping out of line.'

'Yes, no, quite,' replied Felicity, quite dismayed at Counsel's odd mannerisms. 'I find the dynamics of the firm quite strange myself. They're certainly not a typical bunch of lawyers, by any stretch of the imagination.'

'There's no doubt about that.' Geoffrey breathed in deeply; his cheeks suddenly becoming drained of their usual purplish, gout-threatening hue.

'Please excuse me for a second.'

He stood up shakily, holding onto the arms of his chair to steady himself as pine detergent smells reminiscent of the incident with Marina in the broom cupboard filled his nasal passages. He strode as quickly as his uplifting heels would allow over to the large sash window and threw it wide open. Geoffrey poked his head out as if to greet the unassuming inhabitants of Middle Temple and took a deep breath, his eyes popping like a startled fawn's. Drat that Marina, he muttered to himself, his hands clawing at the peeling windowsill paint. He remained there for a full minute without saying a word and refrained from returning to the conference table until he was fully satisfied that only the rich Square Court air and not bleach fumes were flowing to his lungs.

Geoffrey carefully re-seated himself and thumped his chest hard. 'That's better,' he said, without explanation. 'And where were we?' He looked searchingly at Felicity's fresh face, allowing his mind to meander away from the intricacies of the law. She's just like one of those "It" girls, he thought, but with more stuffing between her ears.

'So, Roger tells me that you are fast becoming an integral part of the firm. Congratulations!'

'That's very pleasing to hear,' Felicity replied, reaching for her papers. 'Thank you. I guess they like the fact that I've made them some money.'

'Absolutely. You're good competition for that Dave What's-His-Name as well.'

'Vallely? Well, possibly.'

Felicity wondered when on earth they would discuss Mr Connolly's plight. 'It's always hard to gauge how well one is getting on in a new firm,' she replied. 'Although, my main concern at present is that some bizarre affectation from one of, shall I say, the more robust characters, rubs off onto me.'

'Oh, my dear girl, you shouldn't worry your pretty head about that.' Geoffrey put a reassuring hand on her arm where it lingered for a split second too long to be a platonic gesture.

'Shall we get on?'

'Yes, of course, my dear.'

Geoffrey shuffled through his papers neatly laid out earlier by his faithful clerk. He untied the pink ribbon holding the documents together and stared unnervingly at Felicity. 'I knew there was something I meant to tell you,' he said, replacing the lid on his ink pen. 'That Dave Vallely - that's his name isn't it?' Felicity nodded in agreement. 'I vaguely remember being told something about him.' Geoffrey paused to lean even more closely towards Felicity's neat chest. 'This is in the strictest confidence, of course.'

'Of course,' Felicity repeated, her eyes widening. Geoffrey pumped his chest up in preparation for a monologue (he did the same thing in court when commencing his summing up of a case).

'Apparently - and this was some time ago, mind you - there were some shenanigans at his previous firm. Portshires, I think it was called. Anyway, I can't remember exactly what happened but I think it had something to do with somebody's files going missing. Dave had to leave rather suddenly. In fact, I do believe the senior partner had to frogmarch him to the door and made him hand over the office keys. Dave denied any knowledge of the matter, of course, but all the evidence seemed to indicate that he was the perpetrator of the crime. It was all very strange. Probably nothing to it but I thought it was worth mentioning.' Geoffrey picked up a copy of the Defence lying on the table in front of him before continuing. 'He seems to me to be the sort of man who wouldn't be too pleased at having his nose put out of joint. You might wish to watch out for him.'

'I see. Well, thanks for the advice,' said Felicity, impressed by the old fool's novel chat up lines. Interesting information, nonetheless, she thought, for whatever reason it was given.

Finally, after Geoffrey had spent an inordinate amount of time dropping his pen onto the floor and accidentally stroking Felicity's legs, she was finally released from the old barrister's haunt. During the conference, they had tediously discussed whether or not Mr Connolly should put in an additional claim for the cost of needing sexual therapy and/ or a lady of the night on a continuing basis now that he no longer had a wife to pleasure him regularly. It was a novel argument to say the least and not one that Felicity, somewhat mystified, had ever previously come across. Eventually, feeling most weary, she had left the conference promising to mull over the unusual proposals as Geoffrey stood watching her from his window with an unnaturally sparkling glint in his eye.

*

Two weeks later, Felicity received a call from the Defendant's solicitors in the Connolly case.

'Hi, Miss Garrett?' a self-assured voice enquired at the end of the telephone.

'Yes?'

'It's Adam Goodhew from the Hospital Trust. I was wondering if I might have an off the record chat about Connolly.'

'Of course. Fire away.'

'Well, as you know, we're only four weeks from trial now and rather than both parties incurring more costs in preparation, I was wondering whether you might have instructions to settle for a compromise?'

'I don't have any such instructions,' Felicity replied, clearly annoyed that he should make any such suggestion. 'Mr Connolly's experts are quite adamant that there have been clear breaches of duty on the part of the treating clinicians. I see no reason why I should advise my client to accept a reduced settlement figure.'

Oh, botheration, thought Adam Goodhew, she's one of those argumentative female solicitor types that I was warned about at Law College. His tutor had advised that there was only one way to deal with these women. 'Look,' he said sternly, attempting to assert his authority. 'You know as well as I do, Miss Garrett, that there are great risks for both sides in having the case heard in court. I've seen your experts' evidence and you know you've still got a number of hurdles to cross before you'll ever have a one hundred percent water tight case.'

It was a great folly, perhaps even misguided, to speak to Felicity in such a patronising manner. Git, she thought, I'm having none of this settlement talk.

'Mmm. Maybe,' she replied coolly. 'The problem, well, in fact, it's only your problem, is that your experts seem to be agreeing with mine. That's abundantly obvious from the experts' joint statement. Why don't you take the opportunity now, whilst we're on the telephone, to have another look at it?'

Felicity could hear Adam rummaging through his papers, searching for the document the parties' respective experts had prepared after discussing the case together. The court had ordered that both sides' experts should meet and thrash out the points of dispute between them in an attempt to narrow the issues before the judge heard the case at trial. The intention was to reduce the time spent in court. Sometimes, it worked.

Adam cleared his throat. 'Look, the bottom line is that I'd be willing to recommend a figure of about £175,000 to my client to get shot of the case. Could you take instructions on that?'

'Of course I will but it's unlikely to be anywhere near high enough. I'll contact you with a response within the next few days.'

Felicity smiled to herself as she replaced the receiver. She had been expecting that call. A few days earlier she had received an Advice on Quantum from Square Court Chambers that, she assumed, Geoffrey had written and had avidly begun reading it to see how much he considered the case was worth. But, as soon as she had finished reading the first paragraph, she was startled by its contents. The terminology used was bizarre; it really didn't make any sense at all and she assumed that Geoffrey's feeble grasp of the English language prevented him from conveying his true valuation of the case.

Ultimately, though, by the end of page three, it slowly dawned on her that she might not have been the intended recipient of the document. She flicked to the back page to read the name of its author and saw to her dismay that it had been prepared not by Geoffrey Carter QC but by the Defendant's Counsel, Mr Richard Ling, another member of Square Court Chambers. She guessed that his clerk must have sent it to her by mistake.

Felicity immediately put down the Advice, realising that she was reading the Defendant's privileged document that was clearly not meant for her eyes. Now what on earth should she do? She tried calling Roger for guidance but, when his telephone remained unanswered, she remembered that he was busy preparing for the annual trout festivities. There had been some dark red galoshes that he had seen advertised in one of his fish weeklies and he had hot-footed it down to a shop in Canterbury to make a swift purchase. Marina was out probably buying lard to pad out any slack skin, she supposed, and so her only option was to ask John Forrester for his opinion as to what she should do. Reading the other side's Advice from Counsel had only been in error but it was unlikely that the Hospital Trust's solicitors would be too happy about it; essentially it could ruin their case. Even worse was the fact that The Law Society might have to be involved. She quaked at the thought.

Felicity walked through the winding corridors up to John's room and found "The Globular One", as she had taken to calling him privately, sitting behind his desk giggling over a crossword clue with Sarah, the latter having plonked herself on the edge of his desk, her fat ankles dangling in the air, feet half out of her scuffed shoes. Felicity took some time to carefully explain her quandary to them and, characteristically, John responded by demonstrating huge disinterest whilst Sarah, on the other hand, sat gaping with her mouth so wide open that, Felicity thought, if an orange was popped into her fly-catching mouth the picture of a suckling pig would be completed.

'Just keep it,' John told her, not bothering to hide his boredom with her query.

'I wouldn't if I were you,' oinked Sarah. 'You might regret it if The Law Society found out. Why not take a copy and send the original back to Chambers? Nobody would be any the wiser and you could read the entire document at your leisure later on as well. My guess is that it might prove to be pretty useful in negotiations.'

Turning the newspaper lying on John's desk around, Sarah examined Four Across. ''Night bird that went to sea in a boat'. Three letters. Any ideas Felicity? We're a bit stuck on that one.'

'Owl.'

'Thanks.'

'Anyway,' said Felicity, not wishing to be side-tracked by crossword frolics, 'I wouldn't have thought that what you suggest would be entirely ethical, either, do you?' She was astounded by her colleagues' flippant contributions to her predicament. 'One further point is that I'd rather not get the clerks into any trouble. Whoever put the Advice into the wrong envelope will surely be in for the high jump.'

'That's not your problem though, is it?' remarked John, retrieving his newspaper from Sarah.

'The difficulty is that there is a date stamp on the front cover so I can't even simply return the Advice without a covering letter or something. There's no hiding the fact that we've received it.'

'You're not still bleating on about that Advice, are you?' said John, looking up.

'Forget it!' Felicity shook her head in dismay. It pleased her to see that John was beginning to perspire over the problematic crossword. 'You've obviously got some pressing work to do,' she added, 'so I'll leave you both in peace.'

Felicity returned to her desk and telephoned Mr Ling's clerk to inform him, in confidence, about the mix-up. It was up to him, Felicity thought, as to how he wished to deal with the matter from there on but she did ask him to inform the Defendant's solicitors about what had happened. One important factor, she thought after she had put down the telephone to Chambers, was that at least she would never forget what she had read in those first three pages. Nothing could change that and she couldn't be criticised for making an innocent mistake. In particular, she had noted, with some distaste, that Mr Ling had said that Mr Connolly should be pleased with an offer of £175,000 as it was, in his words, a 'lot of money for a Claimant'. What cheek! What audacity! And how wrong! Further, at the bottom of page two, he had recommended that the offer be increased to £240,000 at a later date and that it would still not represent the full value of the claim. Big mistake.

*

Later that week, Felicity called Valerie into her office.

'Please come in and shut the door.' Felicity waited until her secretary had seated herself before she began.

'I don't think that things are really working out as well as they might, do you?' she asked.

'What do you mean?'

'Well, to cut a long story short, you never seem to be at your desk for more than ten minutes at a time.'

'That's not true!'

'To be quite honest, Valerie, whilst I appreciate that things are pretty lax around here even at the best of times, I do depend upon you to get my letters out so that these cases can be turned around quickly.'

'But!' Valerie tried interrupting but without success. Felicity held up her hand.

'I wanted you to be my secretary because I know how capable you are but your commitment has gone awry, particularly recently.'

Valerie's cheeks flushed. 'I don't know what you mean! I work a damn sight 'arder than most of the other secretaries here!'

'That might well be true but, to be honest with you, Valerie, I've never seen a lazier bunch of heifers in all my life. How this place manages to keep going, I just do not know.' Felicity stopped speaking for a moment as she recalled the Baron's comments to her as they had sat in his bizarrely furnished front parlour. She was still mightily puzzled. What had he meant by saying that 'it's my Elwyn who keeps those buggers afloat'? It was all very odd.

'Anyway,' Felicity continued, pushing memories of that traumatic weekend to the back of her mind. 'I have a proposal. As you know, if I'm made a partner here you'll be paid much, much more, given your greater level of responsibility.

'Ray and me are 'aving a bit of a rough patch if you must know,' Valerie replied, dabbing at her dry eyes.

'Well, I'm very sorry to hear that but I think you should be put in the picture. Valerie, just think of the prestige!' she added convincingly before clearing her throat. 'I was hoping that it wouldn't come to this but I think you can guess what I discovered in the stockroom the other day after you and Dave had been, *let's say*, searching for some old files there.'

Valerie's eyes widened in horror as Felicity slowly bent down to open the bottom drawer of her desk. 'Recognise this?' she asked, whipping out the rampant vibrator. Felicity pressed the "on" button sending it whirring into action. The two girls were momentarily silenced, both mightily impressed by the machine's throbbing action. Once again, its movement was breathtaking and, as Felicity laid it carefully on her desk, it glided from one side to the other pushing pens and paper out of its way onto the floor, aware of its importance over mere legal documentation and office stationery. Somewhat entranced, Felicity let it carry on its merry way whilst she continued her discussion with her secretary, the reverberating sound adding weight to her plea.

'So, Valerie, how shall I put this? Mmm,' she said as she put her head to one side. 'Essentially, if you help me get partnership, then I'll say no more about the little incident in the basement. How does that grab you?'

'You've no proof that it's mine!' Valerie spat angrily.

'You're quite right.' Felicity drummed her nails slowly on the desk. 'But that's not really the right attitude to take now, is it?'

Felicity spun the vibrator round so that it twirled in the opposite direction. 'All I need to do, with your help, is get as much work out as possible every day. That's the way to way to make money and that's the only way that I can think of to impress the partners. So,' Felicity continued, flaring her nostrils in a bull-like fashion at her bemused secretary, 'you just get back to your typewriter and crack on with some work whilst I put this baby away.' Felicity switched off the vibrator, popped it into the drawer and locked it with a key. 'There, all safe now,' she cooed.

DOMINIC

Roger sat at his desk, flicking through *Fish Now!* when he felt a warm vibration beneath his left hand. He sighed contentedly, opened the top drawer and lifted the gold plated receiver. 'Baron?' he said.

'Hello, Rog. How are you this fine morning?'

'Well, Baron, well. And what can I do for you? Everything ship-shape at home, I hope?'

'Yes indeed, apart from having to sell off a few of my favourite artefacts.'

'Oh, dear. I *am* sorry to hear that.'

'Yes, it is a shame but that's why I need to speak to you now, in fact. You see, the Baroness and I 'ave 'ad a bit of a blow.' The Baron paused to dab his unlined brow. 'The camping business 'as suffered quite a loss recently.'

'Oh dear. Nothing too serious though, I hope.'

'Not really but I put a lot of money into developing those new 'ot dog poles. Remember I mentioned them to you last time we spoke?'

'Oh, yes, of course.'

Vivid memories of the Baron's black hairpiece floating through the London sky came swiftly to Roger's mind. It had frightened him a bit. The wig had looked, from a distance, like his mongrel, Patch, to whom he was particularly attached.

'Anyway, my butler - your receptionist - Dominic, without my permission, mistakenly thought that he might like to assemble a tent before the final testing process had been completed and, sadly, just as he was slotting the last "dog" into place the blasted thing exploded.'

'No one hurt, I hope.'

'Not really, although it was difficult to tell, what with Dominic being Scottish, an' all.'

Roger shook his head. 'To be quite honest with you, Baron, it has always been slightly tricky convincing the partners that he is a trained receptionist particularly as no one can understand a word he is saying.'

'I do understand, Rog, I do. The thing is, is that the Baroness, bless 'er sweet soul, 'as insisted that he leave Ty Bach with immediate effect. He's ruined the hallway. It's covered in flakes of pig skin and I've just this minute booted him out.'

'Ah, I see. Well, if it's any consolation he can keep his job here providing the others don't get too fed up with him.'

'Thank you, Rog.' The Baron wiped a tear from his eye. 'I do love my staff, I do, do.'

Roger was bewildered for a moment. Had the Baron said 'doo, doo'? He sincerely hoped not. 'One more thing,' the Baron continued. 'I've decided to branch out into the entertainment business and I've bought myself a little Nightclub just to cheer myself up, you understand.'

'I *do* understand.'

'And I'd like you to be my special guest there any time you can make it. It's called The Purple Rinse Club and I've recently hired a new leading lady who's got some novel moves.'

'Indeed?' Roger's palms were starting to feel quite moist. 'I promise I'll do my utmost to become acquainted with the premises in the very near future.'

'That's my boy, Rog. I knew I could rely on you.'

*

John put his head round Sarah's door. 'Fancy a drink?' he said. 'I think everyone's gone round to *The Bull*.'

'Yes, why not?' Sarah grabbed her coat hanging from a peg on the back of her door and followed John out of the building. Moments later, they settled themselves at a small, round table.

'I can't see the others, can you?'

'No, doesn't look like they're here yet.' John glanced around the room, his eyes seeing only fog behind his scratched contact lenses. 'I wonder where they've gone? Do you want to try round at *The Bung Hole* instead?'

'Let's wait. Maybe they're on their way,' replied Sarah. 'We did leave bang on 5pm, after all.'

'Yeah, maybe. Shall we get a bottle of wine, then? Red or white?'

John took out his moth-eaten wallet and peered into the dark cavity within. 'Have you got any cash on you? My wife appears to have taken mine.'

Sarah bought a bottle of Chianti, returned to the table with two glasses and poured out the wine first into John's glass and then into her own.

John picked up his glass by its stem and took a quick sip. A dark red line coloured the pale skin above his thin upper lip. He leaned in closer to the purple liquor, eyeing it lovingly and inspecting the texture of the liquid that was intoxicating his pickling mind. He took another and then another sip and could feel his hands become weak as the alcohol trickled through his limbs and were soothed by its effects. He felt buoyed up - sufficiently so to question his wife's constant irritation with him. Was he really that much of a let down? A glaze formed over his already blurred vision and he looked at Sarah and grinned stupidly. She wasn't that bad looking, he thought. Different from his muscular wife but not what you'd call ugly. He wondered if she had a boyfriend but didn't dare ask; it would be far too embarrassing for him and it might cause Sarah to think that he was interested in her when nothing could be further from the truth.

'I'm glad the others aren't here.'

'What was that you said?' asked Sarah, unable to decipher the splurge of words that were spilling from John's darkening mouth.

'I wanted to tell you something, in private.'

'Oh, yes?'

'You must promise to keep it to yourself.'

'Of course. Mum's the word.'

John, momentarily forgetting about guarding his personal space, leaned towards Sarah. 'Roger came in to see me this afternoon,' he explained. 'He said that the partners are really pleased with the way that I, with your help, of course, have developed the industrial disease department and they're thinking of offering me partnership next year.' John swayed back suddenly as Sarah's round face became too clear in his fuggy vision.

'That's fantastic news!' Sarah raised her glass. 'Congratulations!'

'And, obviously, that's good news for you in the long term as well,' John mumbled on. 'It should raise your profile within the firm.'

'Oh, I'm not too worried about that at the moment. I've only just started at Meade Pullen so I really couldn't hope for any sort of promotion, anyway.'

'Well, you're wrong there. Roger told me that the partners have got their eyes on Felicity as future partnership material as well.'

'*What?*'

'Yep. They're really impressed with the way she works and the money she's made. Did you know that she's already hit her target for this year?'

'No, I didn't, but I might have guessed as much.'

'Aren't you just a little bit jealous?' John asked, slurping at his last few drops of wine.

'Ha! Not in the least!' Sarah replenished John's glass. 'Anyway, she hasn't made any friends along the way and that's what I consider to be most important at a new firm; she's got to be the most unpopular person at Meade Pullen.'

'That's not how Roger sees it.'

'Do you know what she said to me the other day?' ranted Sarah, not wishing to lose momentum in criticising her fellow female employee, 'I asked her to come out for a drink and she told me that she didn't need to rely on her work colleagues to provide her with a social life. What a bitch.'

'Mmm,' mumbled John. He was enjoying this commentary.

'The thing is, and you know in a way this is good for her,' Sarah went on, 'that she knows exactly what she excels at, i.e. making money, and that's all she wants to do. She doesn't want to go out socialising with the likes of you and me, simply for two reasons. Firstly, she has nothing in common with the rest of us, and, secondly, if she came out with us and had a few drinks we might catch a glimpse of the real Felicity. That, in turn, might have an impact on how she is perceived in the office and, as a result, it might just affect her work.'

John stared at the circular wooden table for a few seconds before looking up at his frizzy-haired friend.

'That's very analytical of you, Miss Kelleher. I'm impressed,' he said, unaware of his oral discolouration, 'and surprised.'

'The thing is, John, you, more than I,' she said licking her lips in case her mouth had also been blessed by the red grapes, 'should know that in order to be made a partner you need to have a special niche to fit. Otherwise you're just bland, bland, bland; the same as everyone else.'

Both John and Sarah fell silent for a few minutes, both privately thinking about Marina and her hidden qualities.

'What have I got then?' asked John.

'Think about it. Who else would go out and get pissed with all those Union reps? You do it because you know that none of the others will. That's what makes you stand out. You don't care who sees you make an arse of yourself.'

As Sarah finished speaking, the pub door was heaved open to allow a cold blast of air into the dark pub room. They watched a man dressed in a kilt lurch towards the bar.

'Is that Dominic over there?'

'Looks like it.'

John saw his fellow employee stagger across the flag-stoned floor. 'Jesus, he looks a bit worse for wear,' he muttered, looking down quickly in the hope that he wouldn't be spotted.

After much stumbling and bumping into furniture, Meade Pullen's finest Scottish receptionist eventually ordered a triple shot of whisky before spending several minutes searching through his worn pockets for loose change.

'Are you sure you want this?' asked the impatient barman, bored with this sallow-faced punter before him.

Dominic repeated the fumbling, rummaging exercise, muttering endlessly about hotdogs as he did so, much to the annoyance of a number of less inebriated customers. 'That bastard Baron!' he shouted.

Sarah stood up. 'Come on, John. Let's get him out of here. It'll be embarrassing if anyone thinks he's with us.'

The two of them took hold of Dominic by his limp arms and guided him out onto Euston Road. The trio stumbled along the pavement until the reassuring sight of a black cab with its taxi sign illuminated appeared out of the darkness from King's Cross Station. Sarah waved her arm and, after the taxi had come to a halt, peeped inside the cab to beg for Dominic to be taken home. The driver shook his head.

'There's no way he's getting into my cab, mate,' he said, his experienced eye quickly identifying his potential passenger's handicap. 'He'll puke everywhere.'

The taxi began to move off. Sarah, desperate to get Dominic off her hands, lunged at the speedily ascending passenger window. 'Stop!' she yelled. 'Look. Here's an extra tenner to pay for any cleaning costs.' She opened Dominic's wallet and, as she did so, a photograph of the Baron together with a note addressed to Roger fluttered out onto the pavement. Sarah flung the wallet containing Dominic's home address at the driver. 'Keep the change,' she barked, bundling the receptionist/butler/driver into the taxi and slamming the door shut.

'What a nuisance!' she muttered, brushing her hands on her coat. She bent down quickly and picked up the note for Roger from the road before John had time to realise what had happened. 'Sorry, John, but I think I'll go home now. Dominic's antics have put me off having another drink.'

John shuffled his grubby shoes. 'Yeah, you're probably right. My wife will be wondering where I am. I think I'd better call her to see if she wants me to pick up some food on the way home.' And then cook supper for her whilst she stamps on my glasses, he almost added. He trundled off towards the Tube station, terrified that he was late and sincerely hoping that she wouldn't sprinkle chilli pepper in his pants again.

*

Sarah, meanwhile, took the Northern Line home. She nestled herself into a seat and, when she was sitting comfortably, opened the letter addressed to Roger and ran her eyes over the Baron's scrawled handwriting.

Dear Rog,

The other day, when we were talking about my problems over the camping empire, I forgot to mention that I might not be able to sub you any more cash to cover your negligence claims. I know this is going to be a blow for you but I've had to part with my last bowl of rubies for a new swimming pool for the Baroness. The last one simply wasn't big enough for her inhuman abilities and now only a hundred metre indoor pool will suffice. Women, eh?!

As a result, I would strongly advise you and your fellow partners to get that Investors In People award as quickly as possible so that your insurance premiums are manageable. You did mention that having Mari (Marina) on board would help your prospects but, trying not to be too indiscreet, her being my sister and all that, I would suggest that you appoint another female partner as soon as you can. As you already know, I have become quite fond of that Felicity girl not least because of her ankles, but also I have noticed that, since her appointment at Meade Pullen, there have been far fewer requests for handouts from you. She may not be Welsh, but you can't have everything!

Hope you and Pamela are well.
Best Wishes,

Baron Von Roberts.
P.S. The Baroness says that the last batch of trout was superb and undoubtedly helped her win the 800 metres front crawl race last week.

Sarah scrunched up the piece of paper and threw it on the floor.

IAN

Sarah reached Clapham South Tube Station and walked back home to Old Town. She called out for Ian as she walked up the once-grand staircase in the house that they shared with five others. Sarah went straight to her bedroom, changed out of her work clothes and wrapped an old stripy dressing gown of Ian's around her before going into the kitchen.

'Hi!' she said, spotting Ian standing in front of the fridge. 'You're here! I wasn't sure when your shift finished this evening.'

'Yeah, I came back at 6.30 to make supper.' Ian leaned over the wooden kitchen table and pecked Sarah quickly on her cheek.

'Fancy a drink?' he asked, pouring wine into a glass.

'Thanks,' Sarah replied. 'Mind you, I've had a few already.'

'Oh, yeah?' Ian laughed. 'With your fancy man?'

'Yes, I was with John but he isn't *my* fancy by any stretch of the imagination.' Sarah pulled the dressing gown more closely around her middle.

'What's he up to then?'

'Well, he wanted to tell me, in confidence actually, that he's going to be offered partnership.'

'That's good news isn't it?' Ian looked at Sarah earnestly. 'I mean, isn't he desperate for the money? I'm sure you told me that he's landed himself with a huge mortgage.'

'But I doubt that they'll pay him much more,' Sarah continued. 'It just means that he's one step closer to equity partnership, that's all.'

'What's the difference, then?'

'Equity partnership is when you get a share of the profits because you own a share of the business but salaried partners are still employees.' Sarah explained, noticing Ian's blank face. 'Basically, it just means that you get your name plastered onto the firm's notepaper and have some involvement with the running of the firm. Salaried partners could potentially be personally liable for the firm's losses if it goes under. I guess it's a tricky place to be but the risk is worth it if you're offered equity quickly enough.'

'Bit harsh though, isn't it?'

Sarah sniffed as Ian roughly sliced up an onion. 'They do things differently outside the police force.'

Ian threw the onion peel into the bin. 'Not jealous are you?'

'Of course not! How could I be? I've only just joined the firm and, anyway, I'm just not interested in stuff like that.'

After supper they lay on their make-do bed in front of the gas fire as it belched out toxic carbon monoxide fumes. All Sarah could think about was the fact that she was about to come in second place again. What was it about her, she asked herself? Why couldn't she ever be the best at something?

As the night wore on Sarah resolved to do something about it.

*

Ian was moving quickly up the ranks within the police force and had made it clear that he expected his girlfriend's career to mirror his own. Ultimately, Ian wanted to marry a provider and have countless bouncing foot soldiers, as he called his future offspring, parading round him in his four-bedroom North London semi. Generally, Sarah didn't feature heavily in these visions of happiness although there was a time, a few years ago, when an unexpected salary raise momentarily placed her in the running.

Ian was an only child; he had never had to share anything in his life and there was no way he would wish to indulge another with what he saw as his just rewards of promotion. When the two had first met, Ian had seen Sarah as a young, lively girl with a bright future ahead of her - exactly the type to interest him. At that time, he was a very junior, mildly good-looking police cadet and it had been relatively easy to grab her attention. All he had had to do was to recommend her services to a few criminals who were desperate to get out of the mess they had landed themselves in and to be provided with sufficient cigarettes to while away the long hours in the cells. However, over the years, whilst Sarah's appearance had vaguely improved, her legal skills had not and his view was that she simply did not have the wit to be anything other than an assistant solicitor. Partnership would never be round the corner. Not ever. For Ian that was not enough.

DAVE

'New suit, Dave?' Felicity raised her eyes slowly from her work and took in the cheap cut of the crumpled jacket hanging from Dave's sloping shoulders as he stood up on the other side of her desk.

'Yeah, actually.' Dave smiled as he ran a stubby finger round the lapels. 'I bought it wiv me bonus. I thought it would be 'andy coz I can wear it for work and then keep it on to go out clubbin' of a Fridee night.'

'Dual purpose then. How clever! So, what can I do for you then, Dave?'

'I just need to take five files of yours to review. It's wot we agreed at that supervisors meeting. Remember?'

'Yes, of course. Help yourself.'

Dave pulled one of the filing cabinets open. 'I think I'll just take the thin ones. It'll mean less work for me to check frew.'

Felicity watched as Dave removed the new cases from the drawer. 'Bring them back as soon as you can,' she said. 'I don't want to have any outstanding post on them.'

'Will do.' Dave turned to leave the room and, with all five files balancing on his left knee, managed to shut Felicity's door.

*

It was 5.30pm. Felicity turned off her Dictaphone, put on her black, fitted coat and left for home. It didn't take long for her to reach Notting Hill Tube station and soon she found herself stomping up the escalators past the lazy oafs who were carried up slowly without having to move their limbs. The entrance hallway soon loomed up before her and she leapt, deer-like, from the last step. It was whilst she was momentarily suspended in mid-air, that she discovered her right heel had become lodged in the metal ridges of the stair and, as she landed, she lurched forward, her stocking-clad foot freeing itself from the ensnared shoe. To her dismay, Felicity found herself lying face down on a pair of shiny black leather brogues and, pushing herself up, she realised that the remainder of the crisp attire belonged to none other than the author of the Advice on Quantum she had recently read; it was the Defendant's barrister, Richard Ling.

'Felicity? Are you alright?' he asked of the girl who lay at his feet.

Felicity turned to see her Prada footwear being mashed against the escalator threshold. It might just as well have been purchased from any high street store, she thought, given its sorry state.

'I'm in a bit of a hurry to get home,' Felicity gabbled. What was going on? Felicity never gabbled, nor did she blush but there was definitely a hot sensation creeping up the back of her neck. Suddenly, it dawned on her that Richard Ling was very, very good looking. In fact, he was *fucking hot*.

'I'm going out to see a film with a friend,' she blurted, desperately trying not to let lust shrivel her mind.

'Oh, right. Well, I'm off home. But I expect I'll see you at court in a few weeks' time. You're dealing with that Connolly case, aren't you?'

'Yes, yes, I am,' replied Felicity as she hopped about, bumping her shoulder pads into fellow commuters.

'See you then. Bye.'

Feeling most disturbed by her chance meeting with such a *gorgeous* man, Felicity hobbled as gracefully as she could manage out of the Tube station. To think that she had spent hours in his Chambers during the Conference with Geoffrey and failed to make inroads with someone so clearly suitable! She must be losing her touch.

Once home, Felicity ran a bath. Just as she was sinking into its soapy depths, the front door was thrown open. It was James, looking particularly flustered.

'Everything alright?' Felicity asked as she watched her "lover" drop his little-used briefcase on the floor.

'No, not at all.' James grimaced, loosening his tie. 'There's been a crisis in Bedford Park and I'll have to nip over to my parents' house straight away.'

'What's happened?'

'Not sure, but Dad said it was an emergency.'

'Oh dear. Shall I come?'

'If you think you can face it, yes please.'

Felicity dressed quickly, ready for action. Only five minutes later they were whizzing their way round to James' parents' home and, on their approach to the Peters' wisteria clad Edwardian house, they could see all the lights blazing. They leapt out of the car and, given the apparent urgency, felt free to waltz straight in to Ground Control (as the Brigadier had aptly named the hallway) without knocking.

147

'What's happened, Father?' James asked earnestly on seeing his father's knitted brow. This in itself was quite a feat as Brigadier Peters had fantastically long eyebrows, so antennae-like that Felicity often surreptitiously placed him next to the radio in order to get a better reception.

'It's your mother, James. She had a spot of bother in Chiswick earlier this morning and she's ended up in gaol. Not sure what to do next. The family solicitor only deals in wills; crime's not really his bag.'

'Why didn't you call Felicity?'

'Well, she's not family and, you know, she is a girl.'

'Yes, I know she's a girl.' James smiled to himself, thoughts of Felicity's snow-white panties filling his mind.

'Who happens to be here,' Felicity explained slowly in case her male companions had failed to understand that that's what being in the same room as someone meant.

'Oh, yes.' The Brigadier eyed Felicity suspiciously. 'Well, what do you think we should do?'

'I think you should start by telling me how Mrs Peters ended up being arrested.'

'Not that straightforward.' The Brigadier wrapped his thumbs around his braces and paced around Ground Control. 'You see, sometimes Mrs Peters doesn't realise that there are some males in this city…' He held up his hand as James loyally tried to speak on his mother's behalf. 'I know it's hard to believe, son, but yes there are some men who don't find her attractive. There we are.' Brigadier Peters shook his head in disbelief. 'We all have to deal with our demons at some time in our lives and I'm afraid your mother's reared its ugly head today.'

'Oh, Mummy!' James cried out, hiding his face in his hands.

'Anyway,' the Brigadier continued, oblivious to James' distress. 'Mrs Peters was in the changing rooms in one of those clothes shops on the High Street when she became stuck in an outfit - a little leather number actually - and called out for help. No one came to her aid and after a while she had to stagger out of the cubicle, still with her arms strapped above her head - the skirt bit was too tight - and into the shop. Sadly the young male assistant took fright and for some bizarre reason thought that your dear mother was making a pass at him and called the cops. Simple as that. She was bundled into a panda car and whisked off to Shepherd's Bush Police Station. Not even Notting Hill, which would, of course, have suited her far better - and then thrown into a cell. Can you imagine?' The Brigadier's eyebrows twitched agitatedly, searching for Long Wave. 'Now what do I do?'

'Let me think. I'm sure I could sort something out.' Felicity examined her manicured hands as she devised a plan of action. 'I'd better speak to the Sergeant at the police station and get Mrs P out of there as quickly as possible. Goodness only knows what she might end up doing if she's left to her own devices. She hasn't taken any of her Sunday Worship items with her, has she?'

The Brigadier turned pale at the thought of the flame-coloured calling cards demonstrating his elderly wife's athletic abilities being handed about the station. 'I sincerely hope not,' he replied.

Felicity picked up her handbag and turned to face the two dimwits standing before her. 'It's probably best if you stay here.'

After some of Felicity's best eyelash-fluttering conversations and Mrs Peters' earnest promises to refrain from unaccompanied clothes shopping, the latter was allowed to leave the police station. Rather fortunately, the young shop assistant had decided not to press charges and, better still, since the leather dress had to be cut off, Mrs Peters was allowed to keep it.

'It might come in handy this Sunday, after all,' she muttered before hopping into a black cab and making her way home to the arms of her rotund husband.

Felicity walked slowly back to the flat, past the rows of expensive shops on Holland Park Avenue and then up Ladbroke Grove. As soon as she had closed the door she saw the answer machine's light flashing. She pressed the "play" button and heard James' round vowels ring out:

'Hi, Fliss, darling, it's me. I'm still at my parents' house and it looks as if I'll probably stay the night. Just one thing though - I need a favour. Father has asked if you might look after Mummy tomorrow. He's playing golf and he doesn't want to leave her on her own after such a traumatic experience. Could you come over in the morning and bring some fresh croissants and royal jelly with you? Thanks, Flissy Darling. Bye!'

'Oh, bugger,' said Felicity out loud. She had not really planned on acting as a nanny to a nymphomaniac for the whole day. She had people to sue and an office to sit in.

CLAPHAM

That Thursday afternoon, Sarah arranged to see a client in Balham just after lunch. There was no point in returning to the office after the meeting, she had told John; she would simply go home and dictate the client's statement whilst it was still fresh in her mind.

After Sarah had left the client's house, she popped into the supermarket to buy some ingredients for the supper she was planning for her sister that evening. She lingered over the packets of salad, worrying whether peppery leaves of rocket were still sufficiently fashionable to sate her sister's fussy tastebuds before finally splashing out on a bag of potatoes to spite her for being so thin. It was, by then, only mid afternoon and so Sarah decided that she had enough time to walk home via Clapham Common. That way, she could save herself the cost of a bus fare although she would have to cross the building site in the back garden in order to reach the rear door to the house.

Sarah strolled along the pathways, taking deep breaths of the fresh, crisp air that blew from west to east over the large expanse of scrubland, muttering occasionally when the bags full of food rubbed against her already laddered tights.

She thought of the black, unblemished, silken hosiery worn by Felicity and decided that she would never again visit the sales to purchase another pair of 40 denier tights in the wrong size. It simply wasn't worth it; walking to work with a crotch perilously near your knees was none too pleasant, whatever the savings.

Finally, Sarah saw the rear of her home in the distance; its imposing roof, despite some tiles having been blown off, rearing up above the loft conversions that surrounded it. She stumbled over the mountains of rubble and, finally, arrived out of breath at the back door. It took only a few shoulder-heaving attempts to force it open and she stepped into a room full of debris left by the builders. Sarah made her way gingerly between the detritus to reach the kitchen door and, as she stood with her hand on the brass door handle, she was sure that she could hear voices. Was one of them Ian's? She couldn't be sure. Sarah held her breath and listened again. All was silent. Sarah opened the door and walked towards the stairs leading to the hallway. Suddenly, she heard the voices again.

'Ian? Is that you?'

There was no reply. The silence was creepy. Sarah felt scared. Any stranger could gain entry into the cold and unwelcoming old house through the back door just as she had done.

'Ian?'

Sarah felt terribly vulnerable but finally glad that she had indulged in numerous pastries. She hoped that her extra bulk might now come in handy. She crept quietly up the stairs to the first floor, tiptoeing so as not to be heard, having placed two of the noisily rustling shopping bags on the floor and carried the remainder up to the kitchen. She then returned, as silently as before, to pick up the bags left at the bottom of the stairs but, as she leant over to reach for their plastic handles, she heard a door creak open below. Sarah froze again. Her heart pounded. There were definitely two sets of footsteps moving around on the concrete floor below. She heard some muffled talking and then, to her utter horror, someone began to climb the stairs from the basement.

'Ian?'

A dark headed person rounded the stairs and Sarah, most relieved, saw her boyfriend's startled face. 'You frightened the life out of me!' she screeched.

'What on earth are you talking about?' Ian asked, his cheeks flushed. 'I've been putting the bins out. More's the point, what are you doing home now? Aren't you supposed to be at work?'

'I've been to see a client who lives nearby and it wasn't worth me going back into the office. I came straight home to cook supper for this evening.' Sarah picked up the remaining shopping bags by way of explanation. 'I didn't see you when I came in through the back door earlier. You gave me quite a fright slinking out of the basement like that.'

Ian scratched his head. 'I've been busy sorting out some of the junk down there. You must have walked straight past me when I was in one of the side rooms.' He put a clean hand on the banister rail and gripped it tightly. 'By the way,' he added, 'I wouldn't go in those rooms down there if I were you; there's all sorts of building equipment lying around on the floor and you might end up hurting yourself.' Sarah looked at her boyfriend.

'Didn't you hear me call out?'

'No. Of course I didn't hear you or else I would have answered, wouldn't I?' Ian pushed past Sarah without offering to help carry up the shopping bags containing his supper. He leapt up to the landing and as soon as he reached their bedroom, he dashed in quickly, slamming the door in Sarah's face and locking it shut.

'Ian? What's going on? Let me in!'

Sarah rattled the door handle as she tried unsuccessfully to open it. 'Who were you with in the basement? I'm sure I heard someone else down there.'

'What? No one. I'm getting changed. My clothes got filthy carrying that rubbish out.' Sarah could hear Ian rummaging around in their bedroom, opening and closing drawers.

'Just let me in.'

'Yes, yes. Hang on. What's all the rush about?'

Five minutes later the door was opened.

'For the last time, Ian, what the fuck is going on?' Sarah marched into their bedroom and stared at Ian in bewilderment. 'And why have you shut the curtains? 'It's not as if anyone is able to see you out there getting changed.' Sarah crossed the room and pulled back the dusty rags covering the dirty windows.

'If you must know, I bought you a present and I wanted to hide it before you got home.' Sarah raised her eyebrows. There was a distinct lack of a present-giving aura about him that she did not fail to notice.

'That's not like you.'

Sarah turned back to the window and looked out across the building site. She rubbed hard at a splodge of dirt that was obscuring her vision.

'Is that Tara down there?' she said, unable to believe her own eyes. 'I'm sure that's her crouching behind one of the fork lift trucks.'

'What?' gasped Ian. 'What are you talking about?' He leapt over to the window. 'Oh, yes, I think you're right.' Ian tried to speak in his normal, disinterested tone as he rubbed vigorously at the windowpane to get a better look. 'That definitely looks like her. Well,' he said coolly after clearing his throat, 'I always said that she was an odd girl.'

Sarah took out her mobile phone from her pocket and pressed speed dial. She watched her sister take out her phone and glance at the tiny screen indicating the name of the caller and then immediately switch it off before hurling it back into her handbag.

THE MISSING FILE

A few days later, Felicity sat on the Tube planning her preparation for the forthcoming trial. Mr Connolly had, on her advice, rejected the Defendant's offer of £175,000 and had simultaneously put forward a counter offer in the grand sum of £300,000. The initial reaction from the Defendant was not positive; the NHS' solicitors viewed Felicity's valuation as ludicrous and unrealistic; the Judge would never accede to all Mr Connolly's requests. Felicity was uncommonly anxious. She worried whether her client would be better off accepting some form of compromise. At least that way he wouldn't be risking everything in court. What would happen if the Judge preferred the Defendant's expert's evidence? Mr Connolly could end up with nothing! Equally nerve racking was the fact that if he lost, she might have a black mark against her name as far as the partners of Meade Pullen and Co were concerned.

Felicity sat staring at the advertisements glued onto the inside walls of the train. She had to remind herself continually of Richard Ling's written advice for the Defendant's solicitors. What figure had he mentioned in it? She tried hard to remember. Was it £240,000? She racked her brain. She wanted to make damn sure that she squeezed every last penny out from the Defendant for Mr Connolly.

After numerous delays due to chewing gum or such like being stuck on the rails, Felicity finally reached the office. She hung up her coat and made her customary cup of Earl Grey tea, (Felicity had learned to accept that the coffee bean was not part of the culture at Meade Pullen) placing her mug on the "Welcome to Bedwas" coaster before turning to open the filing cabinet. The drawers were labelled in alphabetical order and she looked into the one marked C. All that was there were 'Chowdry' and 'Clipper'; the Connolly file was nowhere to be seen.

Felicity picked up her phone and dialled Dave's extension.

'Hi, Dave, it's Felicity. I was wondering if you took the Connolly file to review yesterday when I was out?'

'No. Remember I took the thin "S" files? I put them back in your room. They should be in front of your desk.'

Felicity crossed the small room and threw open all the filing cabinet drawers one by one, pulling apart each and every one of her files, but the Connolly file was nowhere to be seen. Nowhere. Felicity ran over to Valerie's desk.

'You haven't got the Connolly file, have you?'

Valerie, busy typing, noticed Felicity's furrowed brow and pulled out her earplugs.

'Sorry? What did you say?'

'The Connolly file. Have you got it?'

'No, don't think so. Why?'

'I can't find it.'

'Have you looked in the drawers?'

'Of course I have,' snapped Felicity. 'The last time I worked on it was on Tuesday. Remember you did that letter to the court on it?'

'Oh yes. Now I remember. I put it back on your desk when I'd finished. I'm sure I saw it there yesterday morning when you were out.' Valerie raised her hands, ready to type.

'Has anyone taken it to do some work on it?'

'Maybe Roger has it? It was his originally, after all.'

'Yes, well, let's hope so. Could you call his secretary to find out?'

Felicity walked back to her room and closed the door. I'm sure he'll have it, she thought to herself. Stop panicking. Everything will be fine. She started pulling open the cabinet drawers again just in case she had overlooked the file in her haste. She couldn't find it. It was simply not there. It had gone.

Valerie put her head round the door and saw Felicity's worried face. 'Roger's secretary says that he hasn't got the file. He hasn't looked at it since he passed it over to you.' Felicity tore at her hair.

'What on earth am I going to do now?' she cried out in alarm. 'I've got to file a costs schedule with the court by 4pm today.' She looked at Valerie for some much-needed inspiration but her secretary merely shrugged her shoulders.

'Could you go and ask all the fee earners and their secretaries to see if they've got it? I can't begin to stress how important this is. We need those documents for the judge to consider.'

Felicity watched Valerie as she trotted off, transparently keen to wander about the building, and then closed the door behind her. She leant against the wall and put her hands over her face.

'Fucking hell! This is a fucking nightmare!' she yelled. She stood helplessly for a few moments before taking a deep breath. 'What the fuck am I going to do?'

An hour later, Valerie had still not returned and, by this time, Felicity was frantic. Unable to sit down she had paced around her desk trying to work out what could have happened; it was a complete mystery to her as to how a large file containing medical records could disappear so easily. Such a situation was simply unheard of.

Felicity looked at her watch. It was 11.20 am and the bundles were supposed to be in court by 4pm. She was not going to be able to do it.

Finally, fed up with waiting, Felicity charged out of her room and marched straight into Dave Vallely's office without knocking.

'I thought I'd find you here,' she snarled at Valerie through gritted teeth.

'I was just checking that Dave didn't have your file by mistake,' Valerie explained as she jumped off Dave's lap.

'Really? Storing it in his crotch?'

Valerie looked at her errant hand still wedged between Dave's legs and swiftly removed it.

'I was depending on you to help me look for that file. I've been pulling my hair out and all you can do,' Felicity continued, seething visibly, 'is fool around in here.'

'Now, 'ang on a minnit, gurls,' interrupted Dave. 'Squabblin' won't get you nowhere.'

'Look, David,' Felicity barked tetchily. 'You're hardly the innocent party in all this.' Dave's eyes bulged at her in anger. 'Leading my secretary astray and dragging her off to the stockroom.'

'Wot you talking abat?' Dave asked, jutting out his chin aggressively.

'Don't you come all innocent with me,' Felicity spat. 'Any recollection of a vibrating machine?'

Felicity immediately spun round to face her secretary, worried that she might become carried away with thoughts of the object of her desire. 'Valerie, I assume that you haven't found the Connolly file?'

'No,' Valerie answered. She glared at Felicity through narrowed eyes, glutinous blobs of blue mascara causing her eyelashes to stick together in an azure mass at the edges.

'Have you asked everyone about it?'

''Course I 'ave.'

'Well then, go back to your desk. I'll be bringing out some urgent tapes for you to do in a minute, so hurry up.'

Felicity stomped back up to her room, picked up the 'phone and dialled the number for Geoffrey Carter's Chambers. After being placed on hold and subjected to a tinkly version of *Bohemian Rhapsody* for several nerve-racking minutes, she was finally put through.

'Hi, Geoffrey. How are you?' she asked, trying to sound casual.

'Fine. Fine. And, more importantly, how are *you*?' Geoffrey oozed as he lit a cigarette, obviously pleased to have a woman on the other end of the phone by late morning.

'I'm a bit stuck, actually, and I was hoping that you might be able to help me.'

'Of course, my dear girl! What can I do?'

'Basically, and this is extremely embarrassing for me, Geoffrey, I can't find the Connolly file. I've looked high and low and it's simply disappeared off the face of the earth.'

'Oh, dear!' Geoffrey paused to take a long drag from his Sobranie cigarette. 'Has anyone else worked on it?'

'No. I last saw it on Tuesday and then I was out of the office yesterday - I had a personal matter to sort out.' Felicity's mind wandered back to Mrs Peters' inconvenient escapades with the shop assistant that had resulted in a last minute day out of the office. 'But my secretary says she's sure that she saw it on my desk. Now it's just vanished.'

'Look, Felicity,' Geoffrey said calmly. 'Don't worry. I'll get my clerks to bike over all my papers. You can go through them and then take it from there.'

'Thank you so much. I'm honestly at my wits' end.' Felicity allowed a little whimper to escape from her carefully glossed mouth.

'I can well imagine, my dear. I assume that since you're preparing the trial bundles that the Defendants haven't increased their offer?' Geoffrey asked, rubbing his little hands together.

'No, no. We're still miles apart. They're sticking to £175,000 at the moment.'

Geoffrey sighed. He hated having to prepare for trial. It was far too tiresome and, since it would mean that he would have to work on the case that night, he would have to cancel his dinner date with the little minx from Fulham, too. Actually, he thought, recalling her diamond encrusted eyelashes, he was getting to be quite fond of her. 'Well, I'll get onto my clerks now. Please don't hesitate to call if there's anything more I can do, my dear.'

Felicity replaced the receiver and considered the situation. Undoubtedly, after the trial there would be a huge argument about costs and she would need to prepare a schedule of the time spent on preparing the case so that it could be sent to the court. Without her file it was impossible for her to prepare any calculations. If only the firm had a computer system in place, she could simply print out all her old letters and attendance notes. However, this was not so and she felt that she had no alternative but to ring Mr Connolly to ask for copies of all the letters she had sent him. She prayed that he hadn't thrown them away. Her hand lingered over the phone for a few seconds whilst she gathered sufficient courage to make the embarrassing call to her client.

'Fuck! I don't know his fucking number!' Felicity stormed out to Valerie's desk.

'Right. Do something useful and call Union Headquarters for Mr Connolly's number. If they ask why you need it, say we're just checking it for our records. I'm sure you'll think of something. Just make sure that they don't know what's happened. Not yet, anyway.'

Valerie stopped typing and pulled out her earplugs.

'What was that?'

'Just get Mr Connolly's number for me, will you?'

I'd really like to kill you, thought Felicity.

Back in her room Felicity tried to plan how she would, as diplomatically as possible, tell Mr Connolly that she had lost his file. Five years' worth of work. All those receipts and invoices he had sent. All those long letters describing how he was coping since his wife's death. Gone.

'Here's the number,' said Valerie, handing Felicity a scrap of paper. 'By the way, the Union bloke rang. He wants to know what's happening with the case. I told him you'd call him back.'

Felicity took the piece of paper from Valerie and dialled Mr Connolly's number. She told him that someone (not her) had mislaid his file and that it would surely turn up in the next day or so but just to be on the safe side, she would need him to return all the letters she had sent him.

'Sure, no problem,' said Mr Connolly. 'I do hope you find the file though. I gave you the original death certificate and also the last photos I took of my wife with the children before she died. I'd like them back, you know.'

'Of course, no problem. I'll return them to you as soon as I can.' Felicity cringed.

Next, she called Adam Goodhew.

'Hi, Adam,' she said calmly.

Adam smiled to himself on the other end of the telephone. 'So, are you calling to accept the offer?'

'No, sorry, but I do need to speak to you about my costs schedule. I was wondering if you could give me some idea as to how many letters I've sent you?' Felicity explained that she didn't have a computer and then winced as a guffaw, unsuccessfully stifled by Adam, travelled smoothly down the telephone line. 'And I was hoping, rather cheekily,' she continued, writhing in her seat, 'that you might have scanned mine in. It would just mean pressing a few buttons to find out how many I've sent.'

'Sorry, Felicity,' Adam sniggered. 'We don't scan incoming letters. Looks like you'll have to do a manual count.'

Felicity clenched her teeth. 'Actually, to be completely honest with you, I'm having a bit of a nightmare and I desperately need your help.'

'Oh, yes?' Adam knew that catching an opponent on the back foot, so to speak, would undoubtedly put him in a better negotiating position.

'I can't find my correspondence file and it's got all the court documents in it as well. I can probably get copies of the court documentation from Counsel but I'll need copies of my letters to you if I'm going to be able to prepare a costs schedule. It's supposed to be there by 4pm today.'

'I know. I've done mine.'

'Couldn't you ask your secretary to pull out my letters and copy them for me? Please? I'll buy you a drink after the trial ends.'

'Well, what a generous offer! Sounds almost too good to be true!'

'Please? Please? Please?'

'OK. I'll try to sweet-talk her into it. I'm just warning you though, she tends to be a bit of a monster.'

'That would be fantastic. Thanks so much Adam.'

'Oh, don't thank me; don't think that you won't have to pay for my secretary's time.'

Felicity sighed and put down the receiver. She sat back in her chair. What an embarrassing conversation! She had felt like a total jerk, making such a ridiculous request to a blithering buffoon like Adam. Anyway, it was now done and at least she would be able to cobble together a bundle for the court within the next day or so. She would try to explain the situation to the judge if he queried why there was a delay in filing the documents. Sadly, she thought, Judges did not understand or accept explanations for tardiness on the part of solicitors. Good lawyers were punctual lawyers and the common view from the Bench was that if they were indeed any good they would have gone to the Bar. Fact.

THE CONNOLLY TRIAL

The day of the Connolly trial arrived and Felicity, feeling extremely nervous, stepped out of the offices on Gray's Inn Rd and hailed a black cab. As she whizzed south towards the Royal Courts of Justice on The Strand, she thought back to the days leading up to the disappearance of the original Connolly file that, thankfully, she had just about managed to reconstitute with copies of various documents. It was still a mystery as to what had happened; no one had admitted taking it and it clearly hadn't been inadvertently misfiled.

The last time she had seen the file was the day before Mrs Peters' incident on Chiswick High Street and the day after that she had been at the Peters' home in Bedford Park. Well! What a day that had been! Felicity cringed when she thought back to the sights she had witnessed. Mrs Peters, supposedly traumatised by a stint in the police cells, had asked her to sort out her Lost Property box, full of goodies left from a year's worth of "Sunday Praise". (Mrs Peters, never much of a speller - she had other things on her mind - had labelled the box *Lost Propeartee*, much to Felicity's annoyance.) Items that were beyond description were to be stacked into neat piles depending on their size and gender of the likely owner. Felicity had thought that it would be an easy task, but, oh, no! Three hours she had spent in Mrs P's boudoir wrestling with her conscience and occasionally with a selection of the larger pairs of pants. Some garments were so glaringly sadomasochistic that they bordered on the illegal; how would she explain her involvement with such an institution as the Peters' Sunday night fiasco was fast becoming to The Law Society? What she was doing was bordering on handling dangerous goods: coloured plastic toys so bright and enticing that, at first glance, might appear to be more suited to a child's toy box were stuffed into each and every corner of this rampant middle-aged woman's bedroom suite. In fact, thinking back, it had been seriously difficult for Felicity to identify the objects in the darkened room as willies of every colour, shape and size hung from the lampshades, knobs flickering on and off.

Felicity was unsure why she had had to do undertake this task. She had assumed that her role that day would be to bring cups of tea to a disturbed possible future mother-in-law, unfairly accused of exposing herself to a young male. (That's justice for you, she thought.) What was worse was that whilst Mrs Peters delivered the lost property back to her guests' homes situated around the more genteel corners of West London, she had been asked to dismantle the plastic statuette of Mrs Peters so that the cleaner could dust the fiddly parts. During that time, Brigadier Peters had returned from his 18 hole round of golf, forgetting that he had insisted on Felicity looking after his beloved wife in his obligatory absence, taken a shower and then roamed around the house dressed only as nature intended. The sight that greeted Felicity as she entered the kitchen was not a pretty one and the former SAS soldier had had to resort to the protective qualities of a cheese grater to ensure that their relationship was not permanently affected.

*

The taxi cab pulled up outside the courts and Felicity, once she'd paid the driver, clicked her heels over the pavement past the rows of photographers and in through the court's doors. Inside, she plonked her briefcase on a table and waited calmly as a uniformed security guard rummaged through her personal effects, gazing at her with interest after discovering an item left over from *Lost Propeartee*.

'Felicity?' A faint voice behind her spoke. It was Mr Connolly, looking ashen, waiting patiently for his tardy solicitor to arrive.

'Hi.' Felicity held out her hand. 'All ready for this?'

'I think so.' Mr Connolly gulped. Felicity noticed that he was trembling. 'It's a shame I can't smoke in here. By the way,' he added, looking about him at the enormous marble hallway. 'I checked the court listings while I was waiting and we're in Court 4.'

Felicity turned to lead the way up the stone stairs to the first floor and, once at the top, walked around the balcony that ran along three of the four sides of the atrium. Finally, she caught sight of Geoffrey looking vaguely comical as if he had borrowed a cape and a moth-eaten fur hat from his late mother's wardrobe.

'Right, Mr Connolly,' said the eminent barrister authoritatively. 'This is your big day. Let's see what we can get for you.' Geoffrey dabbed at his hot forehead with a monogrammed handkerchief. 'However,' he added, 'as a matter of courtesy, I think we should have a quick chat with the Defendants before we go in. Shall we?' Geoffrey offered his elbow to Felicity as if escorting her to a dance.

Arm-in-arm they walked in a most stately fashion over to their opponents leaving Mr Connolly to sit quietly on his own. Richard Ling stood next to Adam Goodhew and,

Felicity thought, was looking even more dashing than before, now that he had his wig and gown on. She turned crimson, hardly able to speak as she recalled the incident in the Tube hallway and looked down at his brogues noting that they were the same ones that she had landed on. She had touched those shoes, she thought, and nearly swooned.

'Right then,' said Geoffrey. 'Let's get down to business.' He stared hard at Richard, trying to scare him with his hooded, blood shot eyes. 'Would you be agreeable to an off the record chat?'

Adam gave a quick nod of his head in approval and the two barristers wandered down the corridor to talk in hushed tones, full of self-importance. There they stood, only a foot apart, arms crossed, taking turns to mutter into each other's ears before gazing upwards to the high ceiling as if anticipating some Divine Intervention. Unsurprisingly, none came and the two walked back to their respective solicitors, both with their hands now crossed behind their backs.

Geoffrey stood with his feet apart in front of Felicity; his lined brow furrowed with frustration and thin lips pressed tightly together.

'What did he say?' she asked.

Did he mention me? She almost added.

'Well,' said Geoffrey, bowing his head and mumbling out of the corner of his mouth so that the Defendants would not be able to read his lips and so see his (true) response to their proposal. 'They might be prepared to increase to £225,000.' He glanced at Mr Connolly furtively, raising an inquisitive eyebrow. 'They say that they're not prepared to go any higher as it is Defendant Counsel's view that Judge Blewitt, who's hearing your case, is unlikely to be sympathetic to Mr Connolly's requests concerning the children. In fact, Mr Ling appeared before him last week when he was acting on behalf of a Claimant and apparently he had a nightmare getting anything decent for even a straightforward future loss of earnings claim; nothing nearly as ambitious as this one.' Geoffrey shook his bewigged head. 'In fact, I do recall that he made some comment about it in Chambers last week when he returned from his day in court. Furious, he was! *Furious!* Flung his Brief at our poor clerk, he was so angry.'

Felicity took a step back. 'But surely Mr Ling,' *Richard*, she breathed, inadvertently fluttering her eyelashes, 'is worried that the Defendants might be at risk of losing their argument concerning the future loss claim? Otherwise the offer wouldn't be increased at all, I'm certain?'

'Yes, that's my view exactly.' Geoffrey muttered disagreeably, trying to hide his frustration. He did like to get these blasted matters resolved without having to go into court if at all possible. After all, his brief fee would remain the same regardless of the time it took the claim to settle that day and he had been hoping for a free afternoon, nipping up to Ede & Ravenscourt as there had been a really super gold tie on sale there that had caught his eye. Honestly, he thought, rubbing at a scuffmark on his shoe, he didn't care for difficult solicitors who ruined his plans by being tediously efficient for a client.

'Look,' he said, grumpily, as Mr Connolly joined them. 'What I suggest we do, subject to your instructions, of course, Mr Connolly, is to say that we'll accept £275,000. That's roughly about £25,000 less than our maximum valuation of the case and it takes into account the fact that the Judge is highly unlikely to accept all the heads of your special damage claim. Its just being realistic that's all.'

Mr Connolly was momentarily dumbstruck. 'Do I have to say right now?'

'Well, put it this way, we're due to go into court in five minutes so you haven't really got all the time in the world.' Geoffrey's mind wandered back to the gold tie. 'You would, of course, have stood a better chance of getting a higher award if you had listened to my suggestions concerning sexual therapy although, I understand from Miss Garrett, that that was not something that you were willing to entertain.'

Felicity, meanwhile stood racking her brain, trying desperately to recall what exactly Richard Ling had written in his Advice on Quantum. She was sure that the maximum figure he had mentioned in that advice was £240,000. Sure. Felicity put her hand gently on Mr Connolly's jacket sleeve. 'Don't worry about going into court,' she said as her client looked incredulously at his barrister. 'You've been preparing for this day for five years and something tells me that you should hold out just a little bit longer. Don't accept their offer in a hurry simply because the Judge wants to be amused by some amateur performance from the Bar.' Felicity loosened her tightening grip on Mr Connolly's forearm. 'The offer will still be there in half an hour, I'm sure. Take your time.'

Mr Connolly's shoulders relaxed, relieved that blood could still flow up past his wrists. 'Thanks,' he muttered, tears welling in his tired, puffy eyes.

Geoffrey, most irritated by his fussy instructing solicitor, picked up his never-used Civil Procedure Rule book and marched huffily towards the courtroom's doors. Inside, both parties took their seats along the hard pews and, after a lengthy wait, Judge Blewitt entered. All attendants bowed their heads in deference to the man who held Mr Connolly's future in his gnarled, ink-stained hands and patiently waited for the drama to unfold. Unfortunately, the delay was too much for Felicity and, as she sat back down, she began to experience the most dreadful sensation. Oh no! She panicked, her fingers gripping the edge of her seat. This was really not the best time to have one of her flashbacks. Felicity held her breath and tried hard to concentrate on Mr

Connolly's plight; any slip would result in a dive deep into a clinical Black Hole. Boy, she thought, her fingers tightening their hold on the wooden pew, was she glad that she had not gone to the Bar?

Felicity tried desperately to get her thoughts away from any potential disaster by watching Geoffrey place his court book on the floor and then carefully step up onto it. He peered over the lectern and spent a number of minutes clearing his throat before beginning his Opening Speech. 'Your Honour,' he said. 'This is a case concerning alleged negligent clinical treatment.'

Judge Blewitt raised an inquisitive eyebrow. 'Shit,' he said a little too loudly. 'I thought it was a boundary dispute.' He had spent hours, literally hours, reading up on land law and was incensed to think that his new found wisdom was going to lie unused beneath his horse-hair wig. 'Pass me *Cassell on Torts*, quick.'

The Judge was laboriously taken through each and every aspect of Mr Connolly's claim; information so familiar to Felicity that she felt her bored mind wandering back to the episode in the kitchen with the naked Brigadier Peters, his backside looming so large and so hairy that it could easily be mistaken for Hessian matting.

All of a sudden, she was once again back in the operating theatre, this time anaesthetising an unsuspecting (the anaesthetic had worked, after all) patient, her hands clamped tightly around a laryngeal tube when a bored male nurse strapped a plastic penis together with flange onto the top of her head to lighten the proceedings. She had been unable to move at all during the procedure and had spent the following hour adorned with headwear more suited to Lady's Day at Ascot than to administering drugs in a teaching hospital.

'Felicity? Are you alright?' Mr Connolly whispered nervously. This was not the time for his solicitor to pass out on him.

'I think so,' she gulped, touching the top of her head nervously.

'I think I've changed my mind about putting forward the offer.'

'Oh, yes?'

'Could you see if the Defendant will go for £275,000? I really don't think I could take much more of Mr Carter's advocacy skills.'

Felicity bit her lip nervously. 'We'll have to wait until Geoffrey finishes his opening speech and then see if the Judge will let us adjourn.' She looked over at Geoffrey who, she noted, had begun to perspire in the stuffy room.

'Your Honour,' he repeated, 'I am appearing on behalf of the estate of the late Heather Connolly, the wife of Mr Connolly, who sits behind me. It is a claim for damages for alleged negligent clinical treatment suffered by Mrs Connolly at the Defendant Hospital prior to her death on the 30th June 1993. The Claimant's case is that the treatment Mrs Connolly received was sub-standard and resulted in her tragic death. Consequently, her two young children have been left motherless and Mr Connolly has been left a widower.' Geoffrey paused to dramatically shake his head and wipe an imaginary tear from his ruddy cheek. 'As Your Honour is aware,' he continued, 'Mrs Connolly was only thirty five at the date of her death and therefore the claim for her future loss of earnings and the children's dependency is substantial. We shall therefore be hearing evidence both from Mr Connolly and from the parties' clinical experts later in the day.'

Geoffrey drivelled on to Judge Blewitt before finally sitting down to bask in the glory of his golden, rambling words. He turned to Felicity, smiling with such a broad grin that all of his plastic teeth were revealed. (There was a good reason for this display; he had recently had them whitened by a Scottish dentist in Turnham Green and was keen to give them a practice run before venturing out with his little minx from Fulham.)

Felicity was momentarily speechless, recoiling from the display of fluorescent dental work but quickly gathered her wits to inform him of Mr Connolly's wishes. Geoffrey, of course, was thrilled to learn of the change in his instructions and, as the glint of the golden tie in the sale sprang back into view, he leapt up to the lectern to ask Judge Blewitt for permission to adjourn.

Everyone shuffled out into the hallway whilst Geoffrey and Richard (the latter looking marvellous and even windswept for some reason not entirely clear to Felicity) separated themselves from their respective clients and huddled together once more with arms crossed to thrash out the best possible deal for all concerned. They spoke in hushed tones, alternating their gaze between floor and ceiling before returning to their clients. Mr Connolly was led aside to discuss the Defendant's increased offer. They were, Geoffrey informed him, not willing to stretch to £275,000 but were willing to compromise at £250,000, a figure that he strongly recommended Mr Connolly to accept.

Felicity nodded her head, this time in agreement with Geoffrey's proposals. 'It's entirely up to you but I think you should seriously consider their offer. That Judge looks a bit of a tight fisted bastard to me.' Felicity immediately slapped her hand over her mouth, horrified that such blunt observations on Judge Blewitt were revealed so effortlessly. She would have to call her psychoanalyst first thing the next morning; what with the flashback and now this, it was abundantly clear that something dangerous was simmering.

Mr Connolly looked at Felicity. 'You're right, you know. He does look like a tight-fisted bastard and that's what I'm worried about. I reckon I'll take the £250,000.' It was only then, for the first time since his wife's death, that Mr Connolly smiled. 'It's a lot more than I'll get from that old bugger.'

Geoffrey only just managed to contain his glee on hearing such wondrous news. 'A wise decision, Sir. You should feel very relieved that this matter has ended so satisfactorily in your favour.' He stood with his hands placed assertively on his hips. 'You've been exceedingly brave. 'Now is the time to draw a line under the events that happened on that dreadful day in hospital.'

Both parties returned to the courtroom and retook their seats as the Judge was summoned.

'I understand that the parties have reached agreement in this matter. Is that correct?' The Judge beamed, having had the opportunity to partake of his usual mid morning martini that added a certain *je ne sais quoi?* to his judgements.

'Your Honour, yes.'

Felicity looked over at Mr Connolly and smiled reassuringly. Geoffrey continued. 'I am able to reliably inform the court that the Claimant in this most unfortunate action has accepted the sum of £250,000 in full and final settlement. My instructing solicitor has drafted a Consent Order which had been signed by both parties.' Geoffrey paused to hand a handwritten A4 sized piece of paper to the usher.

Judge Blewitt placed his half moon glasses on his hooked nose and read through the Order. 'Let me see,' he said slowly, glancing swiftly at the scribbled hieroglyphics on the A4 sized piece of paper. 'Well, it all seems to be correct,' he remarked, flaring his wide nostrils. In truth, it could have been written in pig Latin for all he knew about drafting documents. 'Now what about costs?'

The Judge had, only a month before, attended a compulsory course on the very subject of 'Costs', in other words the crucial question as to who was to pay the lawyers' fees. It was a hot subject for the Judiciary and, since it was the only bit of law he had any knowledge about, he was damned if some smart-arsed solicitors were going to get paid without a fight.

'Do I assume that since the claim has settled in the Claimant's favour, the Defendants will be paying his costs of the action?' Judge Blewitt asked as he looked over his glasses at Richard, allowing the latter ample opportunity to demonstrate his abilities as an advocate that day.

'Yes, Your Honour. All reasonable costs. I think if I recall correctly, that the Order states as such in paragraph six.'

Judge Blewitt snorted through his nose. 'We'll see about that!' he said, his voice booming over the ushers' heads. 'Whilst I was reading through the trial bundles last night,' (and here the judge was, of course, on dangerous territory as such a practise was pretty well unheard of in the Blewitt household), 'I noted that it was only the Defendant's costs schedule that complies with the court rules. Indeed, I have to say that the Schedule filed by the Claimant's solicitors really is of very little use to me,' he added, shaking his bewigged head and holding the offending papers up high in his left hand. 'I have never before seen such a mass of useless information set out in a court document. I've got a good mind to order each party to bear its own costs. Can you explain this, Mr Carter?'

Felicity felt her whole body cringe with embarrassment. 'I…I…' she stammered hopelessly. Geoffrey whipped round and glared at her. 'Let me deal with this,' he hissed.

'My Lord,' he continued, squirming like an oiled snake. 'I must explain that the Claimant's file has inadvertently gone astray and my instructing solicitor has, in very, very difficult circumstances as I'm sure you will appreciate, used her best endeavours to produce the Schedule that you have before you now. She has, of course, done her utmost to establish the file's whereabouts but it has not come to light, as yet.' Geoffrey leered at the Judge, desperately flashing his plastic teeth again.

'Dear, oh, dear. Whatever happened to good old file management?' The Judge looked harshly at Felicity. 'When the file does eventually turn up I insist that there is an Assessment of Costs hearing. However, I'll sign the Order so that it can, at least, be sealed without amendment.'

Judge Blewitt scribbled his initials on the Order and handed it back to the usher. 'Is there anything else?' he asked.

Richard cleared his throat and stood up again. 'Yes, Your Honour. The Hospital Trust has asked me to pass on its sincere apologies to Mr Connolly and his family for the treatment his late wife received prior to her death. It accepts full responsibility for the appalling outcome and deeply regrets the consequences of its clinicians' actions that resulted in Mrs Connolly's death.'

Mr Connolly bowed his head. Words would make little difference to him now; he had two young children to look after and a house to run. His wife was six feet under.

'Thank you, Mr Ling.' Judge Blewitt turned to Mr Connolly. 'You, Sir, have my sincere condolences too.'

Outside the courtroom, Mr Connolly thanked his legal team and left to take the Tube home. Adam Goodhew, however, recalled the telephone conversation a few days earlier and sidled over to Felicity as she packed up her files.

'Are you taking me out for a drink then?' he asked casually, taking off his glasses to clean them. 'I thought that was what we agreed.'

Felicity eyed her former opponent and, thinking that he looked just like one of the many solicitors whom she had left behind in Southampton, wondered if he was wearing any pants.

'I was hoping that you had forgotten.'

Adam shook his head. Felicity groaned. 'Well only if you promise not to make a fuss about my costs.'

Adam remained silent as he considered her proposition, vigorously rubbing his lenses. 'I'm sure we could come to some sort of compromise,' he said, squinting at her blurry outline.

'Well, how about getting the Silks to do the buying instead?' suggested Felicity, thinking rude de-robeing thoughts about the Defendant's barrister. 'I calculate that you must have paid Richard Ling about £300 per word for his minor performance today and I'm sure that that allows him to treat us to an afternoon drinking champagne at the very least.'

Adam replaced his small, round glasses onto his nondescript nose and peered closely at Felicity. 'Good point, Miss Garrett. I'll speak to him now.'

A few minutes later both Counsel and their respective instructing solicitors walked out of The Royal Courts of Justice with only alcohol and sex on their minds and it took four hours and five bottles of Pol Roger before Felicity and Geoffrey even considered leaving the wine bar. During the afternoon, Felicity had failed to make any inroads with Richard but, although disappointed that her flirtatious efforts went unnoticed, she was at least relieved that he had rebuked Adam's obvious groping beneath the table.

The two barristers returned wearily to Square Court Chambers. Geoffrey headed straight for the clerks' room where, after plucking an ink pen from his top pocket, he scribbled the words *Settled at court - £250,000 plus costs* on the back page of his Brief and chucked it at Archie Salt.

'Good day, Sir?' his obedient clerk enquired after finishing off the last crumbs of his carrot cake.

'Yes, most profitable all round.'

'Out to celebrate now?'

'No, I've been doing that all afternoon with my delectable instructing solicitor.' Geoffrey smiled lecherously, privately recalling Felicity's pert little backside.

'Miss Garrett, Sir?'

'That's the one.'

'Foxy, ain't she?'

Geoffrey raised his eyebrows, surprised by his clerk's unconventional comments. 'I suppose that description might be informative.'

'Not like that fat-arsed girl who came to see you a few months ago. Whatever happened to her?'

Geoffrey turned around quickly to face his loyal clerk. 'Sarah Kelleher? She's at Meade Pullen now, as well,' he replied. 'I put in a good word for her with Roger,' he added, shaking his head. What on earth had got into Archie Salt, he wondered? 'Mind you, it's not clear why he took her on though, by any stretch of the imagination.'

Richard Ling pushed open the heavy door and looked enquiringly at Geoffrey. 'You're not thinking of going home yet, are you?'

'Well, actually, I was. I think I've consumed quite enough champagne for one day.'

'Can't entice you with a little lap dancing just to round off the evening? It would be better than sitting at home in front of the telly.'

'That would depend on which channel you're watching.'

'Of course, of course. But I thought you might be interested in paying a visit to The Purple Rinse Club. You know the one I mean; it's geared towards the more discerning client.' Richard rummaged through his pockets, searching for the club's card. 'There's a new leading lady who started last week and, by all accounts, she's got some novel moves.'

'Really?' Geoffrey and Archie replied simultaneously, their ears pricking up on hearing such interesting vocabulary.

'*Most* novel.'

Geoffrey played with some loose pink ribbon lying on Archie's desk as he considered Richard's tantalising proposition. 'Actually,' he said, 'I think Roger may have mentioned the place to me when it opened. He's a friend of the owner, I understand.' Geoffrey stood up and picked up his brief for the following day. 'But I haven't been there yet, myself.'

'Here,' said Richard as he read out the words embossed in gold on the card. '*Experienced Shimmering Ladies to Tease and Please.* How does that grab you?'

Geoffrey rubbed his eyes. He felt old; even older than the discerning client.

'Sorry, Richard,' he replied, yawning loudly and stretching his stubby arms, 'my feet are killing me. I need to get back to the flat and put them in my home pedicure tub. Maybe next time?'

Geoffrey picked up his keys and hobbled out of Chamber's front door. He hailed a black cab to take him home. There was a lovely bit of pate lurking in his fridge that he had been looking forward to all day. What more could a man ask for, he thought, other than uplifting heels?

PAINTING

'Right then, Fliss. What colour shall I slap on first?' James peered closely at the tins of paint laid out on the newspaper in front of him. 'Salmon pink or Gloucestershire Green?'

Felicity, hair wrapped securely in a lilac silk scarf, bit her lip. 'I rather like both, you know,' she replied, slowly surveying the walls of the living room of their recently inhabited flat in Ladbroke Grove. She glanced down at the out-of-date copy of *Country Decorating* tightly gripped in her rubber-gloved hand. 'Now let me see. I think we agreed on something along the lines of page 56, didn't we?' Felicity flicked through the pages until a photograph of a purple floral sofa on a lurid green background appeared. 'I think this is the look we're after, don't you?' She handed the well-thumbed magazine to James.

'Yes, that's it.' James levered the Gloucestershire Green paint lid up with an old spoon and examined the gloop within. 'Let's get cracking. Pass me the roller,' he demanded authoritatively. James was in fine form that day and enjoying being *Chief of Paint* as Felicity had encouragingly named him.

'So shall we use the Salmon Pink in our bedroom?' she asked. 'It would be a shame to waste it and I think it would be rather calming, after all. We lead such stressful lives, James, that I think we really ought to have a little oasis, don't you?'

'Absolutely, Fliss. I couldn't agree with you more. You know it's all go, go, go with you and me with our hectic careers,' James scratched his nose with the tip of the roller as he reconsidered the words he had just uttered. 'Well, maybe yours rather than mine,' he said before pausing again to deliberate further, 'and so on.'

'And you know my psychoanalyst suggested that I try to relax a bit more?'

'Oh, yes?'

'Yes, remember I saw him last week?' Felicity added, as she twiddled absent-mindedly with the lid of the white spirit bottle. Having anticipated that most of her day would be spent cleaning up James' drips of paint onto the wooden floor she had purchased vats of dilution from the local hardware store in preparation.

'I thought you were having a facial?'

'No, that was the day before. Anyway, I told him about the flashback incident I had in court the other day.'

'Really?'

'He said that it was due to my traumatic rejection from medical college. It's my subconscious memory that's dealing with the failure of it all now; consciously I've clearly got over it.'

'Clearly.' James stirred the green mulch thoughtfully.

'All that hard work being a doctor isn't terribly attractive, is it?'

'No.' James shook his head in agreement. 'I've never been a fan of it myself.'

The couple continued painting in silence, smiling to themselves; each mulling over the marvellous quality of life that they enjoyed. Now and again they turned to look fondly at one another and Felicity even briefly forgot about James' stubbly shoulders resulting from her unsuccessful attempts to shave his wolf-like back.

Three long hours later, Felicity spread out a picnic lunch consisting of cheeses, pickles and the finest varieties of sliced ham on the paint-spattered floorboards. The two decorators sat back to review their hard work as they took a much-needed rest; their skin tinged a sickly green by the light reflecting off the fresh paint.

'Not bad, it is?' remarked James, aware that a splinter had penetrated his jeans.

'No, not bad,' agreed Felicity. 'You know, I've often thought that I might like to be an interior designer. I think I'd be rather good at it.'

'I think you would too, Fliss.' James grimaced. He needed to ascertain the whereabouts of the offending piece of wood and tensed his flabby buttocks as hard as he could manage. 'Ugghh,' he grunted.

'At least I wouldn't have to deal with that hopeless lot at work. You know, James, another three of my files have gone missing.'

'Oh, Darling! What a nuisance!'

'Absolutely! One, in particular, was about a child who had had a misdiagnosed elbow fracture and the others dealt with some pretty sensitive female issues, I can tell you.' Felicity dabbed delicately at her frosted pink mouth with her napkin before chatting on. 'I'm sure you wouldn't want me to go into detail about those.' James nodded his head quickly in response, finding such intimate descriptions most distasteful and drawing the line at the explicit displays in *Vets In Practice*.

'Really, James, it's very annoying to think that someone has been rifling through my cabinets, to say the least, and even worse are the embarrassing explanations I then have to give the clients about what has happened to their files.' Felicity paused to apply some mango chutney to a large slab of cheddar. 'It's as if the tricky cases are being specifically targeted.'

Felicity stabbed at the air, using her knife as a dagger at the imaginary thief. 'You know, James, it's almost impossible to replace all the missing documents. I simply don't know how I'll manage.'

'But the files can't just vanish into thin air. They must be somewhere.'

'Who knows? My guess is that either somebody has got it in for me big time or my secretary, Valerie, is totally and utterly incompetent and has mistakenly stashed them under her desk, which I doubt.'

'Can't you speak to one of the partners about it?'

'I could do but I'd rather they didn't know. Actually,' said Felicity, wrinkling up her tiny nose. 'I had to ask Roger if he had the Connolly file a few weeks' ago but he's probably forgotten about that by now.' She sat back on her heels and popped the cheese into her mouth. 'I'm sure the partners would think that I was batty if I suggested that someone had deliberately taken them. And I can't begin to think what could possibly be gained by anyone doing that. It seems like a lot of reckless effort by someone to achieve very little and all it really results in is me looking stupid and being pissed off. Why bother?'

'Maybe someone wants you to look stupid and be pissed off?' suggested James, helpfully. He wiped his mouth with the back of his hand before gazing at a huge expanse of unpainted wall and picked up his roller. 'Shall we get on?'

Felicity cleared up the lunch plates and returned to rubbing down the paintwork. 'How's your mother?' she enquired politely, changing the subject to something of more interest to James, keen to encourage him to keep toiling away.

'Fine apart from annoying Father by her constant pestering for sex. It's wearing him down. It really is.'

'Poor thing.' Felicity rubbed hard at a particularly thick blob of paint. (It was shocking, she thought, how some people would paint over old layers rather than rub it down properly first. *Shocking.*) 'Has he finished his collage yet?'

'No, actually. I don't think he has. He mentioned the other day that he was having a bit of a problem completing the bottom right hand corner. Apparently, Bernard, the gardener, came across some of his old clippings in the shed that were cut out ready to be glued in place and thought that it would be better if they were burnt rather than Mother discovering them. He didn't realise that the whole point of the collage was to commemorate Evening Worship.' James put down his roller and stood back to admire his handiwork. 'Bernard was a bit frightened, actually, after Father explained that they were only pictures taken of friends and acquaintances. Thought that pressure might be put on him to participate if numbers became low. Anyway, the upshot of it was that he's handed in his notice.'

'I'm sorry to hear that.'

'Oh, it's not too much of a worry. He was never very good with the roses - kept snipping the wrong bits - so Mother isn't tremendously bothered. Says it'll be good for Father to have a workout by tending the garden instead. She read somewhere that the more exercise you do, the greater your sexual appetite. She's got it all worked out, you know.'

187

Felicity continued with her vigorous rubbing as she mulled over James' words. 'I'm sure she has,' she said tartly.

James flexed his biceps. 'Is that why you've got me doing all this redecoration, you little minx?' He raised his eyebrows, meticulously shaped by Felicity who was a dab hand with the tweezers when James was asleep.

'James! I'd never do such a thing!' Felicity didn't dare turn away from the windowsill, careful to ensure that her "lover" did not witness her horror at the suggestion. 'I wouldn't want to endanger your fitness level for the cricket match next Saturday. You know very well that all the best athletes wouldn't dream of any hanky panky before exerting themselves and the same should apply to you.'

'But it's only an old boys' match and it's not for another week!'

'Exactly. You'll be full of spunk by then, and you'll play like a bull in a china shop.'

'What?'

'And no lime and basil crème action either. You'll ruin the new sheets.'

Hours later, after the application of only one coat of Gloucestershire Green, the decision was taken not to apply a second and to always keep the lights on low so that no one would see the bits that had been missed.

THE PARTNERS' MEETING

'All here? Good.' Roger looked around the Boardroom table where John Forrester and the five current partners of Meade Pullen and Co were seated. 'We're just waiting for Mr Hamilton-Hennessy to arrive,' he added, turning to face John. 'He's one of the former partners and specifically asked if he could sit in on the meeting today. You see, he's concerned that Marina might not be able to follow the agenda, being a woman.' Roger put his hand over his mouth. 'Possibly,' he coughed.

Roger surveyed the platters of sandwiches laid out before him still covered in foil. Among them nestled sausage rolls and onion bhajis; each and every item shiny with the whitest lard congealing on their surface. Dusty bottles of water were placed on a sideboard and, next to them, stacked up high, were cartons of orange juice, warming in the July heat. Last of all, Roger noted that the cheese and onion crisps, already tipped out into bowls, were providing a distinctive aroma to the proceedings whilst fast becoming stale in the process.

A few moments later, the door was eased open by a large walking stick and in hobbled Mr Hamilton-Hennessy. He waved his gnarled stick in the air. 'Good morning, everyone!'

he cheered in his fragile, quavering voice. 'How delightful to see you all!'

The "youngsters" stood up in reverence for this remarkable man; the one who was a founder member of this fabulous firm together with Messrs Meade and Pullen (solely for tax reasons had he chosen not to have his name appear in the title of the establishment) and had assisted Roger in manufacturing its relationship with the General Secretary of their Union client, Baron Von Roberts.

Mr Hamilton-Hennessy shuffled over to the table still wearing his bedroom slippers, a trace of egg yolk festooning his collar. 'Hilary!' Roger beamed, holding out a long-fingered hand. 'Please do come and sit next to me.' He pulled out one of the chairs and helped the elderly lawyer ease himself onto the lumpy cushion.

'I remember buying these dreadful items,' Hilary commented, running the tips of his fingers over the armrests. 'Are you lot such cheapskates that you haven't replaced them in all this time?' He stared harshly at the partners who, in turn, looked shiftily at the floor, not one of them wishing to point their finger at the penny-pinching managing partner, Max Hornet. They had, after all, elected him to that role and they only had themselves to blame for allowing him to rule the firm in his northern, tight-fisted way.

'Right, let's begin,' announced Roger. 'Item number One. Dominic McBride: replacement. Marina, what are your views on this?' Marina opened her mouth to speak but stopped as Roger raised his hand. 'Sorry, Marina, but before we start I just wanted to remind John that today he's only here to hear the discussion and that he won't have any voting rights unless, and until, he becomes a partner. In a funny sort of way, his presence here could be viewed as, well, entertainment.'

'For whom?' asked Hilary.

'For himself, of course.'

'Ah.'

'John is fully aware that partnership being offered to him is something that is only being considered by us at present and that nothing is definite. He knows that he'll have to keep up the good work for at least another year before his name appears on the notepaper. His attendance today is merely a taster. Isn't that right, John?'

John nodded his head vigorously, hugely disappointed that he had wrongly misinterpreted the invitation to the meeting and rubbed his hands anxiously up and down his thighs.

'Let's get on, shall we?' Roger turned his slinky body towards Marina, smiling gallantly. 'What were you about to say before I rudely interrupted you?' Marina opened her mouth to speak. 'Well, I…'

'DO YOU UNDERSTAND THE QUESTION?' Hilary asked, slowly enunciating his words as if Marina was from another planet.

'Yes, I was going to say…'

'What he means is whether you think Dominic should stay or whether you think he should go.'

'Yes, I did understand that part.'

'Good, then please continue.'

'Thank you.' Marina smiled at Hilary keeping her lips pinned firmly together. 'My view is that Dominic is utterly hopeless and that really we need someone who can operate the telephone system properly. He is employed as a receptionist, after all.' Marina narrowed her eyes. She was a bitter woman and strongly of the opinion that some revenge was due after she had identified Dominic, in his capacity as the Baron's butler, as the callous informant who, loyal to his employer, had told him about her excessive consumption of sausages doused in olive oil. Not only had the Baroness been livid after learning that her impressive porcine creations were deep within Marina's intestines but even the Baron had been puce with rage after days of hauling fish cakes up to the bedroom to placate the Baroness before she was willing to get dressed.

Hilary gazed at Marina in a fresh light. 'Good point,' he said.

'Thank you Hilary.'

'So,' said Max, ''ow do we go abowt sackin' 'im then?'

All eyes turned to Lucian Tweedle, the employment partner. 'Mmm,' he said, narrowing his eyes as he considered such a remarkable question. 'That's a tricky one. I guess we just pay him off, really.' He rubbed the top of his balding head, misplacing a few long, stray hairs previously stretched carefully across his pate. 'That's the safest bet. Someone could casually suggest that he look for another job. That sort of thing.'

Max leaned over the table towards Lucian as abhorrent thoughts of a large payout sprang to mind. ''Ow mooch would we 'ave ter giv 'im? We don't want to cripple owerselves ower some crappy receptionist.'

'We'll hardly be doing that!' Roger laughed at the ludicrous suggestion, safe in the knowledge that his trout farm would be benefiting from a sharp injection of equitable profits within the coming fortnight. 'More important is who's going to do the dirty deed? You all know that I'm no good at that sort of thing!'

All eyes switched smartly to the floor again, the partners desperately searching the worn carpet fibres as if some lost treasure might be discovered if they looked long and hard enough. Lucian was the first to venture a response.

'It's for the Practice Manager to sort out, being his line manager, I guess,' he suggested. 'Shouldn't we check the Office Manual?'

'We haven't got one!'

'Oh. Well that sorts that one out pretty swiftly then, doesn't it?'

Roger looked over to the Baroness who had been sitting quietly in the corner throughout the meeting.

'Got that Baroness? You'll speak to him, won't you?'

'Yes, Sir. I've made a note of the decision.'

'In short hand?'

'Yes.'

'So that no one else can understand it?'

'Of course.'

'Good.'

Hilary relaxed and smiled. This conversation was music to his ears and, assuming that he had heard right, he remained safe in the knowledge that although in the outside world marked technological progress had been achieved, nothing had overtly altered within the walls of Meade Pullen and Co for the past fifty years. His mind wandered back to the days when he would sit at his desk and watch the world go past as he dictated long, drawn-out letters to his trusty secretary. It had not even been necessary for him to hold a Dictaphone; he had just let his words of supposed wisdom run away with him and then hoped for the best. How the letters and writs had flown from his snapping, twisting lips! How incomprehensible had his statements of case been! And now, as he sat in his creaking chair, how he admired the Baroness' dextrous skills as memories of hieroglyphic-filled notepads flitted through his addled mind.

Roger, meanwhile, felt sufficiently relaxed to sit back in his chair and survey the proceedings. 'Ah,' he breathed. 'I do like a quick decision. Let's move on swiftly.' He took a sip of sparkling water from his glass and looked down at the handwritten agenda. 'Oh dear! This will be a controversial one. Computers. Do we link ourselves up or not?' The glorious smile from one so resplendent with dentures was instantly snatched away from Hilary's face, his eyes widening in horror at the unthinkable.

'Never!' he yelled as he struggled to his feet, waving his walking stick wildly in the air. 'Over my dead body! I will not allow those monstrous creations into my firm!'

'Hilary, Hilary.' Roger repeated the former partner's name soothingly in an attempt to placate him. It worked for babies, he thought, and why not for someone who was at the other end of the life spectrum? 'The difficulty that we face is that we are now the laughing stock of our competitors. We simply cannot go on any longer with our heads buried in the sand. We have to face facts however repulsive they might seem at first.'

'But 'ow mooch will we 'ave ter spend? All those computers will cost oos a fortune!' Max thumped the table with his fist.

'We're well aware that we can afford them; we've all seen last month's billing figures. Just think, Max, if we play our cards right with these machines, then it may well be that we can decrease our secretarial workforce. Think of the savings we'll make!'

This discussion was clearly too much for Hilary. What on earth was happening to his beloved firm, he asked himself? What was wrong with the way he had managed the firm for all those years? It had been all right, hadn't it? They had all skipped along merrily, hadn't they? Issuing the occasional Writ if need be at the local court and chatting courteously with the opposing solicitors about myriad extensions of time for service of documents to ensure that cases never reached trial. Hilary had made a handsome living out of dabbling with the English legal system that way; delays in progressing a client's claim meant that everyone (apart from the client) was happy, happy, happy. Now, all that seemed to remain of those wonder years was the cake trolley pushed around by that marvellous woman, the Baroness, who, he had been told, even made the delicacies herself. God damn it, he thought, his fingers tensing with each vision of the past that flooded into his shrivelled mind, these new fangled partners had even installed central heating!

Max continued to shake his head. 'A'm no way convinced abowt sooch massive expenditure. You'll 'ave to do some serious persuading to get me to agree ter this one.' He leaned forward to scratch his tweed-clad backside before nestling back into his warm seat.

'Put it this way,' continued Roger. 'Last month we had a near disaster with one of Felicity's files going missing. She couldn't prepare a costs schedule because there were no copies of any correspondence and the Judge nearly ordered that each party bear its own costs even though she'd won the case.'

'That's appalling! How could that happen?' demanded Tarquin, the divorce partner, making use of his favourite and most often-used question, his blonde curls bobbing agitatedly around his face.

'I don't know. But if we were networked up - I think that's the right expression - she would have been able to reprint the lost correspondence.' Roger looked anxiously at his fellow partners. 'Something has simply got to be done.'

'And what is more is that I only found out because Geoffrey happened to mention it to me over a drink last week. He said that he was placed in quite an embarrassing position by the lack of a decent schedule, particularly because he was in front of Judge Blewitt.'

'Golly! Don't tell me that that tight-fisted old bastard is still on the circuit?' said Lucian, 'I thought he would have dropped dead long ago.'

'No, he's still sitting on the Bench, steeped in alcohol,' Roger explained. 'I guess it's the pickling that keeps them going for so long.'

The group fell silent as they considered the proposition. It could be their own future, too, sitting with the judiciary in a land where incontinence pads reigned supreme.

'Where were we?' Roger finally asked after he noticed that his fellow partners were drifting off dreamily. 'Computers. That was it. Are we for or against?' Roger cast a sharp eye over at Max.

'Don't yew luke at me for support with yewer silly ahdeas. A've already given yew ma opinion on t'e matter.'

'But just think of the pornography you could view at lunchtime! From the comfort of your own office, and from your own revolving chair! What could be better?'

'Well now. Since yew put it like that, Roger, I might well 'ave to reconsider my position.'

Max narrowed his eyes as he considered Roger's proposal. There might be some merit in it, after all, he thought. His wife, Mrs Hornet, might be pleased, too, particularly if it meant that her evening hour of soap viewing wasn't continually interrupted by Max's crude interpretation of entertainment that tended to include young, Swedish ladies.

'And what is your view, Marina?' Roger asked, safe in the knowledge that Marina was a progressive sort.

'I'm all for it. Not for the pornography, of course, but I can see the merits of being linked up to the real world.' She wiped away a trickle of sweat heading south between her breasts; it was hot in the panelled room and her thighs were starting to stick together as well. She pulled her tent-like skirt up to reveal her tattooed ankles and to allow more air to circulate around her sweltering, hippopotamus sized body. 'Ah, that's better,' she sighed.

'Well, I think that's settled, everyone.' Roger beamed. 'We'll be up and computer literate within a month.'

'But you haven't asked for mine and Tarquin's views!' exclaimed Lucian.

'No need. Majority vote. Job done.'

'Oh.' Lucian picked up his ballpoint pen and, as he did during most partners' meetings, drew the shape of a heart on the bottom left hand corner of the page before colouring it studiously.

'Next up is the question of prospective partners.' Roger turned to John. 'You've already heard our views on your position, so just listen quietly to the next discussion. Obviously, none of this is to be repeated.'

'Of course,' John muttered, blushing again. What would he be able to tell his wife who was sure to give him a grilling when he got home, he wondered anxiously? She would be livid if he failed to provide a full blow-by-blow account. What evil would she inflict on him this time? Hopefully not another night spent sleeping in a cold bath of water. It had been very difficult to explain his shrivelled skin to Sarah the following day. However, with partnership apparently within his reach, his wife might finally be pleased with her choice of husband. He desperately hoped so. His nerves were in shreds.

'I think we're all agreed that, after John, Felicity is the next in line for promotion. Yes?' Roger looked around the table.

'She certainly pulls the mooney in and that's wot we want.' Max started perspiring heavily as he dwelt on his favourite subject. 'She's already stook in twelve grand this month.'

'But does that necessarily make her partnership material?' asked Marina.

'As far as a'm concerned, it's all that matters. We want people like 'er ter stay, don't we? If not, we'll go owt o' business quicker 'un a flash and that's no good fur anyone, a'm sure yew'll all agree.' Max tapped his pen on the table and, crossing his hairy arms, he leant back in his chair, tipping its front legs upwards.

'I guess that's fair comment,' piped up Tarquin and, shaken by his sudden temerity, he immediately looked down at his knees.

'But do you think she could manage with a partnership role?' Marina pressed the partners as she fanned more cool air round her thighs. 'We all know that Felicity works damn hard and makes a lot of money but it's important to remember that she's still very young and may not be ready for such responsibility. How old is she, Baroness, 25 or something?'

The Baroness looked up grumpily, not wishing to be interrupted from jotting down new cake recipes onto her note pad. 'About that,' she muttered.

'The only other thing that bothers me, lovely girl that she undoubtedly is, is that she's been misplacing files,' Roger added, trying desperately hard not to dwell on Felicity's shapely ankles as now was definitely not the time for cravings. 'It's all very odd, you know. Files simply shouldn't disappear, as they seem to with her, particularly not just before trial. And there have been others too, I understand.' For only the second time in his life, Roger was totally serious. 'You know, I suspect foul play.'

'But she's never mentioned any of this to me.' Marina dabbed feverishly at her chest. 'Looks as if she's losing her grip on things. Doesn't bode well for her future if that's the case.'

'Mmm. You may well be right.'

'I think the best thing to do would be to monitor her progress and the missing files situation over the next few months.' Roger looked over at John. 'And what are your views on Felicity becoming a partner?' John's eyes widened as the question took him by surprise. He had been thinking about lunch and was beginning to salivate but cleared his throat before speaking.

'I don't really know her, to be perfectly honest. She doesn't make much effort with the Union members and they are our clients, after all.' He licked his lips as he caught a glimpse of the delicacies laid out for lunch warming on the sideboard and starting to curl at the edges. 'Sarah, on the other hand is always out with them, buying drinks and having a laugh.'

Steam blasted forth from Max's ears. 'I 'ad no ahdea that we employed clowns at sooch high expense,' he snarled. He was not overly keen on any frivolity in the office unless it involved him and was a precursor to sex with a secretary. 'All ah know is that Investors In People expect us ter 'ave some more wimmin's names on t'e notepaper and unless our dear Roger 'ere is happy to oblige us with a sex change,' he laughed heartily at his own joke, 'then we'll 'ave ter 'ave more wimmin partners, whatever they're like. Sarah, Felicity, Auntie Tom Cobbly, whoever. I don't give a moonkey's. Just get 'em on.'

'Did I hear rightly?' bellowed Hilary, his face puce with rage. 'Women partners! Whatever next! It's bad enough with just one,' he said as he pointed the rubber end of his stick accusingly at Marina, 'and there's more bollocks on her than a bull.'

Roger turned to the Baroness. 'Have you got that minuted?'

'Of course.'

'Marvellous.' Roger clasped his hands together. 'I suggest that we take a short break to enjoy our sandwiches and then carry on in fifteen minutes. If we haven't finished eating we can carry on regardless. I'm quite sure we'd all like to end this meeting as quickly as possible.' The entire group nodded their heads vigorously, for once in unanimous agreement with the Chair's proposal.

Roger immediately stood up and thrust the aluminium plate at John. 'Would you mind handing these round, please?' John, eager to help, immediately took the tray and passed the flaccid sandwiches, consisting mostly of mayonnaise, amongst the eager party.

'Delicious!' exclaimed Roger, scraping some pickle from his chin. 'Eat up, John. There's no point leaving them to waste.'

John, already struggling with a weight problem, piled his plate up high. He was a compulsive eater and would, undeniably, have turned to bulimia nervosa had he been able to face stuffing his podgy fingers down his throat. He just loved eating, despite the straining leather belt worn tucked beneath his drooping midriff. John was forever keen to advise his colleagues that his waist size had remained the same since his university rugby days and now wore his belt much lower, allowing it to claw painfully at his hips, five inches lower than its intended position just so that the buckle would not have to be let out a couple of notches. Indeed, he was always irked to find little red pinch marks above his y-fronts when he removed his trousers that, sometimes, whilst he slumbered peacefully, his wife highlighted with a black marker pen purely to while away the twilight hours.

Roger watched as John nibbled away, rabbit-like, at his sandwiches. He kept his head low, only a few inches above his plate, his eyes darting over the table, narrowing frequently with annoyance when someone else picked up a sandwich he had fancied.

'You're a greedy pig, aren't you, young lad?' Hilary commented loudly across the room. John blushed.

'So,' said Roger, once again taking control of the meeting as the trays of food gradually emptied. 'Where were we? Ah, yes. Next on the agenda is the Christmas party. When, where and how much do we spend?'

'Actually,' piped up Marina, 'Dave Vallely has booked *The Blushing Widow* for the last Friday in October. It was already taken for the final weeks running up to Christmas so there was no alternative really but to have it then.'

'But then it's not really a Christmas party, is it?'

'No, but no one will mind if it's early. It's the same every year, remember?'

'Well, I suppose that having it on a Friday is a good thing as at least that way we won't have staff coming in with hangovers,' Roger commented, casting a quick glance over at the thrifty managing partner.

'But on the other hand,' argued Max, 'will it encourage them to drink with gay abandon on booze that we'll 'ave to pay for? They might put a lid on it if they think they'll 'ave ter get oop and coom ter work the next day. A'm not keen on paying for a whole load o' folk ter get blind drunk courtesy o' me and my partners as you can well imagine.'

'Yes, I can well imagine,' repeated Roger.

'How about we limit the amount we spend per head?' suggested Marina.

'Yer daft bird. We do that anyway.'

'How about we tell the staff that we'll only pay for half a bottle of wine each and they have to pay for anything they want after that?'

'Sounds fair enough to me.'

'Got that minuted Baroness?'

Roger looked down at the final point on the agenda. 'And finally,' he announced, 'do we or do we not contribute towards a headstone for 'Backstabber' Elwyn Roberts?'

'I 'ad no idea that 'e'd coughed it.'

'June 29th was the sad day that he passed away. The death certificate mentions an overdose of carrots being the cause. In fact, before his final day of service I did mention to him that I thought he was developing an orange hue to his skin but, well, he was never one to listen to reason.'

The Baroness snorted loudly in the corner. She'd spent years feeding that mean bugger of a brother-in-law and was in no way sorry that her baking had played a major part in his downfall. It was only five days ago that Elwyn had been crushed at London Bridge Station whilst attempting to board a train just before midnight. He had leapt into the darkness, convinced that the extra carrot cake he had consumed would not only improve his eyesight but also give him the ability to hop like a rabbit. His bounce had led him smack into the wall of the Royal Mail carriage whereupon he had slithered down onto the railway track.

As a result, however, the Baroness could now save a fortune on her weekly grocery bill without Elwyn being around and the extra would come in very handy now that the Baron's inventions were not performing as well as planned. She glared across the room at Marina, narrowing her eyes as thoughts of the sausage episode once again sprang to mind.

Roger continued to speak after a brief period of silence. 'I'm sure you're aware, Max, that he worked loyally at Meade Pullen for over forty years.' He spread his thin hands out on the faux Louis XV table. 'I thought it was appropriate for us to send flowers.'

Max rose from his chair, steam blasting out of his flapping, hairy ears.

'You did wot?! Fook me. Why doon't we just pay for the whole flamin' service and be doon. I paid that fat blerk far too mooch when 'ee were alive and there's no fooking way a'm paying a penny more.' Max stood up and scratched vigorously between his legs. 'Right then,' he said. 'If we're all done, a'll be off fer a waz.'

After Max had left the room, John noticed that there was a small amount of pineapple juice remaining in one of the cartons and poured it into a plastic cup. He took a sip, swilled it around his small teeth and then smacked his sticky lips together. So, he thought, this is what goes on in a partners' meeting! And to think that he had frequently worried that the high powered conversation might be too cutting edge for him to understand and that the partners would use long difficult words with masses of syllables! Huh! Talk of carrots instead of the lengthy discussions of mergers and back room deals that he had envisaged! Unwittingly, he stared directly across the table at Marina's cleavage, by now so beaded with sweat that her whole vast decolletage resembled a flash-flooded Cornish fishing village.

THE LAGER FRENZY

It was a hot, hot day, one of many at the very end of an Indian summer. John pulled on his old school cricket whites, admiring his rotund visage in the bedroom mirror before driving over to Acton Cricket Ground for the Rabley annual match against The Lager Frenzy Boys, as they called themselves, from Hubblebury School. He was looking forward to another closely fought contest against his old school's rivals and pictured himself smashing his personal record of 103 runs. Kapow! He could feel it in his bones. All the glory that he constantly craved would be there after just a few hits, a few smashes. His mind was on important cricket matters when he turned into a side road and unintentionally mounted the pavement much to the consternation of a little old lady as he whipped the fragile skin from her elbow.

'Bugger!'

His wife would be livid if she had to fork out for a new tyre again, and he could do without a personal injury claim against himself as well. What with all the scrapes he had had, getting insurance was becoming a tad tricky.

John parked the old Citroen, one wheel still on the pavement, and checked his appearance in the mirror.

He ruffled his hair to make it look thicker and cover his developing bald patch before going in search of his old chums. The Badly Rableys were, as their motto aptly demonstrated, *a force unto themselves* and were renowned throughout the old boy cricket circuit as being fair but slightly dim, always unwittingly allowing the opposing side to win as a result of incompetent scoring. However, these chaps were always so agreeable; the sort who would help your old granny across the road provided that they hadn't run her over beforehand, of course.

John, always the fretful type, was first to arrive at the cricket pavilion and, as soon as he entered, a little frisson of excitement ran through him when he saw to his delight that the tea had already been laid out. He walked slowly around the table examining its contents and planning his next meal, high tea, his favourite. Yum, yum.

When John reached the plate of sandwiches at the far end he simply couldn't resist the cute, Lilliputian fragments of bread that beckoned at him. After checking left and right to ensure that no one was watching, he carefully eased up the Clingfilm and removed a ham and pickle isosceles triangle. He popped it straight into his mouth, whole, and chewed as quickly as possible.

'Hey!'

John swivelled round, experiencing a tickling sensation in his oesophagus as a crust, caught up with his rotating momentum, headed south to rejoin its wholemeal companions.

'Great spread!' a tall opponent exclaimed. He looked at John. 'Did your wife prepare the food?' John looked down at the floor, swallowing the last remnant of sandwich in one gulp. 'No, I can't claim the praise, sorry.' The best his wife had ever given him before a match was a swift kick in the pants, make no mistake.

'Worth coming just for the tea.'

'Yes, that's how I see it, too.'

'By the way, I'm Freddie Blofeld,' the tall man held out his hand. 'Captain of The Lager Frenzy.'

'Gosh! Any relation to the great man?'

'No, sadly.' Freddie shook his head. 'Wish I was though.'

'Yes, me too.'

The two cricketers, not knowing what to say next, stood at either end of the trestle table with hands on hips, nodding their heads and admiring the Victoria sponge.

'Love those cakes. Make life worth living.'

'Absolutely. They do it for me every time.'

'Yes.'

'Yes,' said John, now keen to impress the opponent bearing the same surname of his all-time hero, pulled out the end of his belt to try and move the buckle a few notches tighter. He moaned quietly as he felt his stomach fighting hard against the evil leather restraints. How it longed to hang free.

The other members of the opposing side soon arrived and, after a surprising amount of limbering up for a so-called friendly match, a coin was thrown and the Rabley crew elected to bowl first, their tactics being that they would get everyone out by tea so that they could relax over a slice of parkin and a nice scone smothered in jam and clotted cream.

John ambled out into the sunshine and, after leaning his trusty bat, passed down from father to son, against the pavilion (guarding the cakes) he strode forth onto the cricket pitch. Oh! What a glorious day! he thought cheerily. Standing with legs wide apart he placed his plump hands on his knees. He fiddled with his cap, trying to work out where "extra cover" should stand.

Crack! The ball sailed high in the sky, again and again. The Lager Frenzy lads were scoring runs with gay abandon; the Badly Rableys were in serious danger of losing the cup, *their* cup. John seethed quietly, desperately hoping that Sarah wouldn't make an appearance as she had promised and witness his awful fall from grace. He pulled his cap down further over his forehead to protect his eyes from the glaring sun and saw the ball being catapulted yet again in the opposite direction from where he was fielding. 'Bother!' he said aloud, his frustration mounting as, even after the first few innings, his involvement in the game still amounted to nil.

John straightened up, momentarily distracted by a muscle strain developing in his left arm and winced as he rotated his shoulder forward and back to loosen the apparently stiffening joint. 'Ah, that's better,' he said to himself, seeing the cricket ball fly once more over his head.

He looked about him at his fellow fielders and noticed in the distance that Sarah was getting out of her sister's sports car. John watched as she carefully closed the passenger door and then waved goodbye to the rear of Tara's car as her sister whizzed off down East Acton Lane. He noted that Sarah was wearing sunglasses again and supposed that they were to hide the dark rings that had been developing around her eyes as of late. Sometimes her dark brown eyes were puffy, too, and a bit on the red side. Must be all the late nights she was having out with the Union lads that were doing it, he assumed, and thought that he would try to stay out with her a bit longer in future. Can't be pleasant for a girl to have to deal with all those incessant crude jokes, after all, John decided. Perhaps he should ask his wife for a remedy for her condition? It was never really satisfactory for a girl to have a face like a pie.

The third batsman was now in and John watched as yet another tall chap (what did they feed them on at Hubblebury? Testosterone burgers?) sauntered across the pitch towards the stumps, the ends of his old school tie fluttering gently in the breeze.

'Right then, now for a little action!' John rubbed his hands excitedly up and down his thighs. The pressure was full on now, particularly if a work colleague had travelled to watch him play. He looked over at Sarah again and saw that she was talking to someone. He held his hand up to shield his eyes from the glare of the sun and saw, to his horror, that it was Felicity with whom Sarah was now deep in conversation. What the fuck is she doing here? What if his wife got to hear about the female audience? John quaked at the thought.

However, John had no option but to put this vexatious matter to the back of his mind; there was no time for debate as play had resumed. Crack! The bat struck the ball, once again sending it high into the September sky. This time, it's mine, it's mine, thought John, desperate for the adoration that might result from the capture of an opponent's ball before it hit the turf. He began running backwards, his belly jiggling around like Humpty Dumpty's, completely out of sync with his nimble legs. His hands were held high, cupped, waiting for Deliverance.

As the ball approached, the sun, floating like a giant molten orb, momentarily blinded John. He heard the crowd's cheers of joy and excitement and felt a thrill run through him as he realised that the "Man of the Match" title was now, finally, within his reach. He searched upwards, looking desperately for the ball again, begging for a cloud to obscure the sun's rays. 'It's yours, John!' someone shouted from afar. An intense rushing noise that filled the air. John put his hands over his head. The ball hit his chest and fell flat to the ground. Plonk.

'Aah!' wailed John in fury. He lunged at the ball that had so cruelly taunted him all day and, scrabbling through the short grass towards it, stumbled and fell. He kicked his legs in the air like an upturned tortoise, then turned to pick up the ball before hurling it at the stumps, desperately clawing at the portals of glory. The ball bounced ten yards from its intended position and came to a halt at James' feet.

'I think I've sustained an injury,' John yelled, rubbing frantically at his chest. He waved and staggered back to the pavilion, momentarily too bereft of the anticipated adulation to take advantage of a clear run at the cakes for tea.

Sarah ran over. 'Are you alright?'

'I think so.'

John gazed at Sarah's blotchy nose and sighed heavily. He sat silently for a few moments, reflecting on the afternoon's event, as Sarah blocked out the rays from the sun in front of him. He peered up at her. 'Would you mind passing me a little Battenburg? I think it might help ease the pain.'

'Of course not.'

John watched Sarah slice the cake and place a large section on a paper plate.

'Here you are.'

'Thanks.'

'Marvellous bit of play out there.'

'I'd like to think that I did my best.'

'I meant the batsmen.'

'Oh yes, of course. That's what I meant, too.'

After enjoying the slice of Battenburg, two cups of tea (milk, no sugar), three iced buns all topped off with a glacé cherry, two more triangles of ham and pickle, a pink fairy cake and a yellow Fondant Fancy, John was ready to lie down in the long grass and take a much-deserved nap. He crossed his feet, placed his hands prayer-like on his inflated chest and soon drifted off to sleep.

John didn't stir from his resting place for the remainder of the afternoon. Only occasionally was he brought to semi-consciousness by a fly entering, examining and leaving his open mouth as he snored, twitching his aching limbs, oblivious to the large storm clouds that were gathering above.

Eventually, even without John, the match progressed as predicted and The Badly Rableys were declared all out for 97 runs. Cheers of joy ran though both teams, the losing Rableys glad that another humiliating season was over and generously congratulating their winning opponents heartily as the Heavens finally opened. Large raindrops fell from the sky spattering the brim of John's cap and slithered onto his cheeks as he lay heedless to the storm around him.

The remaining batsmen ran towards the pavilion, bar one. James saw John lying comatose on the grass, oblivious to the downpour and tiptoed over to him before shaking him gently by the shoulders. 'Excuse me,' he said loudly. John woke with a start seeing, to his horror, the face of The Lager Frenzy batsman who had struck the final blow to his hopes and aspirations of becoming Man of the Match. He gasped for breath as a fly was sucked into his airways.

'Wake up! It's pissing down!'

John wiped dribble from his chin, pushed himself up onto his elbows and, once he had regained his senses, staggered to his feet and walked over to rejoin the rest of his losing team, unaware of the grass stains striping the back of his trousers.

Sarah greeted him with a cup of tea as his wet feet sloshed over the wooden floorboards. 'Are you alright?' she asked. 'I could see that you were having a rest so I didn't like to bother you.'

'No, I'm fine now, thanks.'

James, having spotted John now back inside, wandered over from the trestle table with a buttered scone in his hand, leaving Felicity to chat with the Hubblebury captain. 'Nasty blow you had out there,' he said. John jealously eyed the sweetened bun in James' hand, hardly able to concentrate on his fellow companions, so mesmerized was he by the thought of adding a small dollop of jam to the semi-naked cake.

'Sorry? Yes, I had a bit of a shock.'

'So, um, Felicity tells me that you work at Meade Pullen,' continued James, trying his best to be polite to his girlfriend's work colleague.

'Er, um, yes, that's right.'

'Felicity is so glad she moved there from Southampton. She seems to be doing quite well from what I can gather.'

'Actually, we don't see that much of Felicity; she's always got her head down,' Sarah explained, noting that John had his mind on other matters.

'Not in the managing partner's groin, I hope!' added James, a little too quickly.

'No, not that I'm aware of.'

Felicity floated over in her pretty, bias cut lilac skirt, her delicate pumps hardly making a sound on the wooden floor.

'Hello, John,' she said. 'I see you've already met my boyfriend, James.'

'Yes, yes. Didn't know you had a boyfriend.' Felicity wasn't carrying a plate, John noted immediately. What had she eaten? Or what was she planning on eating?

'Have you had any tea? Can I fetch you something?'

'No thanks, not yet. We had quite a big lunch so I'm not that hungry.'

'Oh? What did you have?'

'Well, let me think.' Felicity scrunched up her nose and looked up at the ceiling as she tried to describe the creation James' mother had thrown together at lunchtime.

'Ratatouille, I think, or maybe it was soup. Not really sure which. And salad. That sort of thing. Most enjoyable.' In fact the meal had been anything but pleasant. The day before a session was always a troublesome one for Mrs Peters who, quite literally, got her knickers in a twist about the schedule of events for the following evening.

'So, um, is this Mrs Forrester?' asked James, nodding towards Sarah.

'Good God, no!' John gasped indignantly, leaping deer-like into the musty air with horror. 'My wife is at home,' 'baking bread', he almost added but realised that anything could be further from the truth. Hanging a noose above the marital bed was far more likely.

Sarah glanced out of the window and then put down her plate. She smiled at Felicity. 'My sister has just arrived to give me a lift home. I'll have to dash. See you on Monday?'

'Yes, I'll be there.'

'Thanks for inviting me along, John. I've really enjoyed myself.'

'I'm sorry your boyfriend couldn't make it.'

'Yes, me too.'

'Maybe next time?'

Sarah pulled her dark sunglasses back down over her eyes. 'Maybe.'

John watched as Sarah got into the low sports car. Inside, she disentangled the straps of her handbag from her ankles and turned to look at her sister's perfect profile.

'So, what did you get up to this afternoon?' she asked innocently.

'Just a spot of window shopping along Westbourne Grove.'

'Buy anything?'

'No, I haven't got any spare cash at the moment. Whatever I earn is going towards my holiday in Mauritius.'

'How lovely! You didn't tell me you were going travelling! When are you off?'

'Six weeks tomorrow. It'll be mid summer there by the time we arrive. Boiling hot. Can't wait.'

213

'I bet!' Sarah smiled to herself as visions of tropical beaches brimming with white sand filled her mind. 'Who are you going with?'

'Sorry? Um, just a friend from work. Someone you don't know.'

Tara pulled up outside Sarah's home in Clapham and sped off into the distance as soon as her elder sister had closed the car door behind her.

THE CHRISTMAS PARTY

It was the 31st of October and great excitement was in the air at Meade Pullen and Co. The annual fancy dress Christmas party had arrived and Season's Greetings abounded amongst the staff and blended merrily with the ghostly howling of those who had decided to celebrate Hallowe'en instead.

Participants of this celebratory spectacle had either adorned themselves in unflattering costumes or, if feeling particularly self-conscious, opted to clad themselves in their usual glittery party gear. Consequently, depending on whether it was Christmas or Hallowe'en that was being celebrated, bosoms were tortuously squeezed into clothes more suitable for dwarves or delinquent children. Body-hugging Lycra grappled courageously with wildly wobbling wodges of midriff. There was a smile on every face, even on Max Hornet's. He had uncharacteristically splashed out on a Father Christmas wig and beard especially for the event but this had more to do with protecting his shiny head from the chilly, October air than with any goodwill towards his staff.

Roger strode forth dressed as an eighteenth century gent, complete with top hat. Had the clock been turned back three hundred years there would be nothing to suggest that he was anything but a successful lawyer, coolly swinging his pocket watch as he sauntered along to a late afternoon rendezvous with his mistress. It was interesting, thought Felicity, how her colleagues chose to display their alter egos on such occasion. In fact, what indeed was Roger celebrating? Christmas or Hallowe'en? It was unclear to Felicity, as it was to Roger; the outfit had been all that Pamela could find in his wardrobe apart from fishing garb and his favourite sequinned dresses.

Earlier that evening, Sarah had arrived at Felicity's room just before 5 o' clock with the intention of dragging her from her desk and off to the party. However, this task had been tricky; Felicity had discovered that yet another file had disappeared even though she hadn't been out of the office. Such a disappearance, in itself, was odd as she had found that files generally went astray if she was absent from work for any reason, for example if she was out at court or away seeing a client. Over the past few days she hadn't moved from her desk and usually only Sarah and Roger bothered to stay at the office later than her.

'Shit!' Felicity yelled eloquently in the stillness of her dingy room. Her search for yet another missing file had meant that she had hardly enough time to get changed into her witch's cat outfit before had Sarah arrived, dressed as a reindeer.

'Golly, Sarah, you look most convincing!' she exclaimed as an antler became lodged in one of Felicity's cat ears. 'Look!' squawked Sarah, extracting the tip, her voice muffled by the reindeer's muzzle. 'My tail lights up!' And indeed it did.

The two animals made their way down the road towards the party venue, swiping at small children who continually pestered them with the vexing question 'trick or treat?' Eventually they reached *The Blushing Widow* and immediately ordered some wine.

The gaggle of partners soon arrived at the party venue keen to spread joy and goodwill amongst their loyal staff for all the hard work they had performed during the year. It was a happy moment for all at Meade Pullen and Co.

'So 'oo the fook are yew supposed to be then?' asked Max Hornet as he stood between the two girls and threw his arms around them. 'Pussies?'

Felicity's nostrils flared wide. 'Only in your dreams,' she replied, wishing she were a champion spraying Tom cat.

Max threw his head back, laughing loudly to reveal his inflated tonsils. He assumed that Felicity was flirting with him and consequently ploughed into the conversation by talking about himself. 'Did I mention that a've bought an 'ot tub?'

'No. Do tell.'

'Me un t'e missus spend hours in there. It's fantastic,' he added, shaking his head, not able to believe his good fortune. As the head honcho in the business he was able to spend his weekends sitting in a heated, bubbling wooden cask whose contents could quite easily be converted into mulled wine if only a sachet of mixed spices were thrown in. 'You know, girls, oonly the oother day, we 'ad soom friends rownd and guess what, Felicity?' He nudged her hard with his rhino-skinned elbow.

'You know, Max, I simply couldn't.'

'You would 'ave looved it. We 'ad champagne and them canapé things - sausages on sticks with cheese. We did think about pineapple but then thought, eh, fook it, let's splash owt an' 'ave sausages instead.

'Golly! What an event! And to think that you didn't even invite me! I'm most hurt.'

'Eh, oop. Maybe next time. You keep your costs oop and, you know wot, you might well be there sooping next ter me on soom soonee soomer night. Noothing could beat that, eh?'

Felicity looked at Max. She was confused. Had he said 'souping'? Did he mean that there would be lumps of potato and broccoli floating around Mr Hornet's nipples, whilst they supped pink Asti Spumante? She sincerely hoped not.

'Absolutely, Max. I've always said that there's nothing better than eating outdoors.'

Max grinned. 'Anyway, girls. A'm sorry but a'm going te 'ave te love yer an' leave yer. A'm in demand and a've been told by my fellow partners that a've got ter mingle.'

Max ambled over to a group (or was "clutch" the correct term, Felicity couldn't be sure?) of secretaries standing near massive bowls of chips dunking deep fried slices of potato first into a bowl of mayonnaise and then into another containing tomato ketchup.

'Ooh, I shouldn't!' giggled Valerie, sneaking a dip. She had sewn toffee apples to the edge of her short skirt and could feel that they were beginning to melt in the warming atmosphere.

Max gripped his beard and wrenched it upwards. ''Oo's furst fer a Christmas kiss un a cuddle?' he bellowed. 'Santa's presents all round!' He licked his lips in preparation for an active workout.

And weren't they the lucky girls, each getting a slobber from the man who paid their mortgages every month? They lined up, one behind the other and puckered up for Father Christmas.

Over in another corner, beneath three coloured balloons with the words *Happy Birthday Max!* printed on them, John was busy setting up a Karaoke machine. 'La, la, la, la, la,' he shrilled in his flat, monotone voice. (He had mistakenly been convinced from an early age that he had an ability to sing. In reality there had been a massive shortage of choristers in his parish and the priest, a family friend, had been a desperate man. A lack of ten year olds had led to John being placed in the back row of the choir. Church attendance numbers had started to dwindle at that point.)

'Right then!' John's voice boomed. 'Who's first?'

He looked eagerly around the barren room. Felicity had expected it to be filled with festive tinsel and glittery paraphernalia but, apart from the few balloons, it was decorated solely by a fake silver Christmas tree that had undoubtedly spent much of its youth in Max's hot tub. No one stepped forward to volunteer.

'Come, come now. It's Christmas! Time to celebrate!' John yelled, just loving every moment that he was in charge of the proceedings, guessing that that must be what it was like to be a managing partner. The feeling of power was magic. Sheer magic. He fondled the microphone lovingly, swaying in time to his own, imaginary, music.

'OK, OK, if you insist. I'll get the ball rolling.'

John's globular body shook with excitement like an electrified amoeba as the music to Kool and The Gang's *Celebration* started up. His voice boomed into the room, the hired ivy green elf outfit straining at the seams and partially restricting his ability to perform all the "big" notes. In fact, it took some time to persuade him to leave the stage but, eventually, those staff who had had their cranial synapses sufficiently numbed by alcohol were also able to demonstrate their singing abilities. Even Roger gave an impressive rendition of *My Way*, much to the delight of his fellow partners who knew it could never be so.

Throughout the evening Felicity sat on her perch. She saw Marina, dressed as Minnie Mouse, standing on the sidelines, surveying the proceedings. It was anybody's guess as to why she had chosen to dress in such an outfit; the elephant sized ears did nothing for her spherical face and the polka dot skirt, splaying out like a tent, surely could have housed a family of homeless Christmas elves.

Suddenly, though, through the darkened room, Minnie lunged forward, keen to be in the spotlight. She took hold of the microphone in her small, white, gloved hands and massaged it gently. It was just how Walt Disney would have liked it, guessed Felicity as she watched her mouth the words to *Smack My Bitch Up*.

The music ended but Minnie kept on whirling, ignorant of the outdoor clerk's plans to sing *It's a Long Way to Tipperary* (he was from Ireland and homesick so it was understandable), and it took some time for her to come to a complete standstill. When she did, however, she made it abundantly clear that there was no way that she would leave the stage without a fight and hung on in the spotlight until Roger coughed loudly and strode forth, top hat in hand.

'Come along, Marina, it's someone else's turn now.' He gripped the thick flesh peeping out from beneath her puffed sleeve, enveloping her elbow and narrowed his eyes angrily when she stuck her "Minnie" heels into the linoleum floor. 'We'll have to pay for any damage,' he warned. There were fish to feed out of his share of the profits and he wasn't keen to fork out for skid marks created by a reluctant rodent instead.

'Look Roger,' said Marina in her sober, "fairy" voice, 'I've something to tell the staff at Meade Pullen and I think the best time to do that is now.'

'Oh, Lord!' Roger muttered, clutching at his cotton handkerchief and mopping his brow. 'Whatever next?'

Marina whipped the microphone back out of Roger's trembling hands and took a deep breath. 'Happy Christmas, everyone,' she said, waving a strand of purple tinsel at a few of her favourite colleagues. 'It's a very special evening for us all tonight and it's wonderful to see you all enjoying yourselves so much.' Marina's voice faltered as one of the two remaining balloons burst behind her. 'I know that I'm with all my friends here at Meade Pullen and I think it only fair to advise that, as a result of my personal preferences, I have decided to call myself Meredith and from now on I should be addressed as "Sir"'.

The crowd gasped.

'Oh, fucking hell. That's all I need,' huffed Roger. 'Minnie Mouse in charge of the party proceedings.'

Max who, at the time, was engaged in some very oral banter with a large breasted secretary, spat out his cheap wine across the dear girl's cheek causing beige foundation to trickle down her neck. 'Boogger me' he yelled as he wiped his lip-sticked mouth, 'that's ower Investors in People award up the swanny. We'll 'ave no flamin' wimmin on t'e notepaper. Now, wot'll we do?'

'Gosh, yes that is a problem,' Tarquin added, always being close to Max. 'And one that was particularly hard to foresee. You'll have my full backing on this one, Max.' 'Darling,' he almost added but caught himself just in the nick of time.

'Eh, Roger,' shouted Max, in his gentlemanly manner. 'Wot were the name o' that bird yew said was makin' oos money?'

'I think you're referring to Felicity,' Roger replied as he breathed in sharply, having just spotted one of the young assistant solicitor's velveteen covered ankles, twisting in a circular motion as she sat at the bar.

'That's the one. Well, I reckon we'll 'ave te ask 'er to be a partner sooner than she thinks if that Marina is planning to 'ave a willie stitched on.'

'I presume that the happy event has already occurred.'

'Oh, fook me.'

'Marina, sorry, I mean Meredith, probably could. Perhaps you might care to ask?'

Max seethed, his Father Christmas wig nearly lifting off in anger. 'An' yew can booger off too, yer flamin' poof,' he spat.

Momentarily, Roger was, as they say, caught between a rock and a hard place. The dilemma he now faced was whether to organise an emergency partners' meeting or try to persuade Marina to have her willie de-planted, if that was the correct terminology. Neither seemed entirely reasonable given the celebratory festivities that surrounded him. The fact that Lucian, Tarquin and, for that matter, Max, were seeing double deterred him from suggesting a meeting at this point in time. Some apple bobbing by postroom goblins had caused mayhem and allegations of cheating were abounding *The Blushing Widow's* lower party room. The decision he took that night was to leave smartly without any of the other partners noticing and nip off to the Baron's new lap-dancing club that had recently opened up in Marble Arch.

Roger started walking towards the illuminated exit when he was drawn unexpectedly to those damn ankles again. 'Oh, bother!' he muttered aloud, turning to their owner. 'Would you like to come dancing with me?'

Felicity put down her glass and took Roger by the arm. 'I'd love to,' she replied. 'See you on Monday, Sarah.'

Dave Vallely stared in disbelief as the senior partner escorted Felicity out of *The Blushing Widow*. This time,

Felicity had gone too far; she had outstripped his costs by at least £50,000 and made him the laughing stock of the First Floor. She had even blackmailed his girlfriend by kidnapping the entrancing vibrator. No one should be allowed to do that and think that they could get away with it lightly.

*

As the party reached its natural end and dwarves and elves were thrown out onto the streets of King's Cross, Sarah made her way back home on the Northern Line. It was the last train south and she had only barely managed to keep her cool as her tail was continually switched on and off by the Hallowe'en revellers. Eventually, she arrived at Clapham South Tube station and, after prancing in reindeer fashion out of the tube station, she galloped down the road causing myriad car accidents behind her as drivers mistakenly assumed that her brightly lit rear end was part of a new traffic system. Finally, she reached the large front door, pushed it open and fell inside. She called out to Ian but there was no reply and, given that it was past midnight, she assumed he must be asleep.

Sarah stumbled forward, her footsteps silent in her padded hooves and, just as she was about to walk upstairs, she noticed that the strip lighting in the basement was on. The half bottle of wine generously purchased by the partners of Meade Pullen had been bolstered by a number of Bacardi and Cokes and she felt brave enough to investigate the lower floor on her own. What would a prowler do, anyway, if faced with a reindeer? The worst that could happen, she assumed, would be that she might be mistaken for a long lost extra from *Trigger Happy*.

Sarah tiptoed into the kitchen and stayed there for a while, listening to the mice scuttle around the back of the units, before feeling decidedly silly standing in the basement with her tail light flickering on and off intermittently as its battery began to fail. She decided to go to bed to sleep off her thick head and lumbered back round to the bottom of the stairs.

She was just about to place her front hoof on the stone step when she spotted the door to the scullery maid's old bedroom that was tucked beneath the banisters. She undid the bolt at the top of the door, eased it open and saw immediately that someone must have been in there very recently as the latest *Hello* magazine lay open on the floor. She untangled her antlers from the loose electricity wires dangling from the ceiling and padded into the tiny room, immediately tripping onto a mattress lying on the floor. Sarah fell forwards and, unable to right herself immediately given her cumbersome outfit, sat quite still for a few moments in order to catch her breath before preparing for her final heave upwards.

As her breathing started to slow, Sarah looked about her and ran her hands delicately over the bed cover. Her eyesight blurred in and out of focus as she swayed gently in her inebriated state but something about the cover caught her attention. She peered at it closely. Slowly, it dawned on her that the pattern looked familiar; it was her old Brownies sleeping bag. She bent down and picked up the quilt with the tips of her right finger and thumb, catching sight of a shiny object that lay beneath it. There, twinkling innocently on the Brownie's smiling face, lay the diamante necklace she had given Tara.

*

After the singing had died down and his audience dried up, John had packed up the karaoke machine and gone home to the arms of his beloved wife. That was what he would tell his work colleagues, anyway. In fact, he had leapt on the last train travelling north to his home in Kentish Town and had fallen soundly asleep. Three times that night he had voyaged back and forth between Arsenal in the north and Wimbledon in the south before he was finally awakened by a kindly cleaner keen to remove any unwanted stains from the tube seats. Sadly, by that time, the karaoke machine had been stolen by unkind youths and a beard and glasses had been drawn in blue ink on John's round face.

When he finally arrived home his wife threw a suitcase containing his cricket whites from their bedroom window and refused to allow him entry either into his home or otherwise. He later described it as being a pleasant evening all round.

THE QUEEN OF HEARTS

Roger helped Felicity into the black cab before seating himself next to her and placing his top hat carefully onto his bony knees.

'There's no chance that you would have a willie stuck on, is there?' he asked cutting to the chase. Felicity had hardly curled her tail around her when this strange question was posed. She thought back to the incident in the operating theatre. 'Not intentionally, no.'

'What do you mean 'not intentionally'?' This was a worrying response from such a sensible girl.

'Well, there was a time, a few years ago, when I was a medical student that a plastic penis had been positioned on my head for a few hours but that's the only occasion that I can think of.'

Roger breathed a sigh of relief, gazing at her ankles to reassure himself. 'Did it have a flange at the base?'

'Yes, in fact, it did.'

'Ah, I know the type you're talking about,' he replied, nodding his head sagely. Pamela had a collection of willie paraphernalia at home which she kept hidden behind lock and key, not wishing her golf club friends to stumble across them when partaking of tea at the Wilbraham-Evans household. 'Well, that might resolve rather a large problem we're currently facing at Meade, Pullen and Co, what with Marina's exposure, if that's the correct term.'

Roger wiped away some of the condensation that had formed on the window and peered out at the hotels on Park Lane as they whizzed by. 'We're not far, now,' he said, brushing imaginary dust from his breeches, 'I thought you might like to visit The Purple Rinse Club tonight. It's relatively new and I'm hoping that Geoffrey might be able to join us. He's never been there before, either.'

'I'm sure it'll be fun.' Felicity pulled at one of her ears, feeling marginally self-conscious in her Christmas/Hallowe'en outfit. 'Won't I look a bit odd dressed as a cat, though?' she asked.

'Oh, no one will notice, I'm sure. But you'll have to make it clear that you're not part of the performance, that's all.' Roger tapped at the driver's shoulder and asked him to pull over. He looked at Felicity. 'On the bright side, you never know, you might make some money.'

'Maybe I should take off my tail?'

'No, don't worry about that. Here we are!'

The taxi stopped outside the illuminated doorway of The Purple Rinse Club above which the words *Land of my Fathers* were written in large orange/brown letters.

Felicity slinked out of the taxi and followed Roger through the entrance and into the darkened room. He ushered her towards a circular table positioned immediately in front of a large stage.

'Is this some sort of strip joint?' Felicity asked.

'No, of course not my dear. It's lap dancing, that's all. Quite innocent, I can assure you. In fact most of the ladies who entertain - shall we call it - are grandmothers just keen to make a few extra shillings to pay for their toe nails to be clipped. Or something like that anyway, maybe new teeth. Who knows?'

Roger patted Felicity's velveteen knee gently to reassure her and then, with a flourish, pulled out his wallet heaving with equitable profits, from a compartment within his top hat. Roger, although unaware that the Baron was in any financial difficulty, not having received the letter intended for him (it having been disposed of by Sarah), was pleased to think that he could repay the firm's benefactor by attending his prestigious nightclub. Roger's intention that night was to spend, spend, spend, particularly since he was accompanied by the stuff that his dreamiest of dreams were made of: those darn shapely ankles. With a flick of his wrist he summoned a waitress resembling a member of the Women's Voluntary Institute and a bottle of fine wine was ordered.

'Nothing for you to worry about,' he added, his eyes glinting ominously at Felicity.

Roger placed a £50 note into the decrepit attendant's leathery hand and watched as it was tucked into a snugly fitting surgical stocking. He turned again to Felicity.

'There's just one matter that I need to discuss with you before the performance begins.'

'Oh, yes?'

'Do you remember what you asked me during your first interview?' Felicity looked bewildered. 'It was about partnership and when we might be able to offer it to you. Anyway, if you're still interested, then we'll have to have a serious discussion about it at the office on Monday. I just need to finalise a few details with the other partners, that's all.'

Felicity was ecstatic. Had she heard correctly, she asked herself? Partnership! She couldn't believe her ears and pinched her velveteen thighs to make sure she wasn't dreaming. 'But what about John? Do you mean that I'll be made a partner at the same time as him?'

'John who?'

Felicity looked at Roger earnestly and shook her head. 'Never mind. We'll discuss it on Monday.'

'Right then,' said Roger as the lights dimmed. 'We're off!' A spotlight twirled around the room momentarily lighting up the bewildered faces of the eager audience. Ultraviolet lights flashed on and off making the merry clientele, smiling joyfully, look like crazed corpses anticipating some morbid form of sexual gratification before their final decay, their teeth the only form of identification.

Finally, after five long minutes, the spotlight came to rest on the piano player dressed head to toe in green velvet, with hems of orange braid. He raised his hands high in the air and then, without further ado, struck up *The Girl From Ipanema*. The crowd went wild! 'Hoorah!' they shrieked from every corner of the room. The pianist, buoyed by the crowd's enthusiasm (by day he played at a funeral parlour so this lot made for a pleasant enough change), trilled incessantly, displaying his abilities to the extreme. At one point he even, very cheekily, took a sip of his Sarsparilla with one hand whilst the other dabbled with a boogie-woogie version of *What's New Pussycat?* The pianist was in his element and the crowd unstoppable. They shuffled around to ditty after ditty, occasionally forgetting that the night's main attraction hadn't even begun. Eventually, in an attempt to calm down the aged audience, the pianist - Cremation Chris as he was known, professionally - performed a final flourish and then bowed low.

'More, more!' The crowd screamed, but to no avail. The Master of Ceremonies stood up and took hold of the microphone.

'Ladies and Gentlemen,' he bellowed. 'And now for tonight's feature performance.' The audience hushed obediently. 'May I introduce you to The Purple Rinse's production of Alice in Netherland?' With cloak in hand, he swooped away dramatically and disappeared just in time before a deluge of dry ice vapour belched out from a hole in the side of the stage. As the vapour finally settled an assortment of ladies brazenly stepped out from the bowels of the theatre to the rapturous applause of the audience. Once again, the crowd erupted. Arms were stretched forward at full length as they attempted fruitlessly to stroke the wrinkled ankles of the Netherland Babes. Old these performers may well have been but there was no mistaking that they were also a most feisty lot, all held together with pins and girdles.

'Splendid, splendid!' gabbled Roger, his watering eyes on pins, as he gripped the edge of the table. 'I don't know how much I can take of this!'

On cue, Alice appeared, cute as a Koala bear and twice as nimble. She tore off her clothes until eventually all that was left was her pinafore and eponymous hair band nestling in her blonde, bouffant hair. Notes were thrown at her, hither and thither, in the desperate hope that the blue and white checked pinafore would be whisked away, but to no avail. This lady had eyes for one man alone. She spied Geoffrey entering the forum and was instantly intrigued. She beckoned to him as he made his way through the manic customers clawing at the cast and sat down quietly next to Roger.

'It's a bit dark in here,' he said politely, loosening his tie and attempting pleasant small talk. Geoffrey had had a busy day in court and had hoped for a quick chat with his old chum rather than a jam tart thrust under his nose as soon as he asked for a drink.

'Can't talk now.'

Roger was beside himself, his eyes never lifting from the stage.

'And how are you, Felicity, my dear girl?'

'Very well, thank you.'

'And do I spy a new outfit?' Geoffrey asked, spotting the cat's tail.

Felicity was scarcely able to speak. She, too, was hypnotised by this mystical world of ageing Mad Hatters and Tea Parties. But where was The Queen of Hearts, she wondered, looking around at the cast anxiously? Surely they couldn't leave her out of such a magnificent production?

'Very nice it looks on you too.'

By now Alice, who, by virtue of her unsagging knees, was clearly much younger than her stage contemporaries, had walked down the steps leading from the stage. She gyrated her hips before Geoffrey in a manner he had only witnessed in his wildest of dreams.

'Madam,' he said, clasping the arms of his chair tightly. 'I am an Officer of the Court and I find your actions most disconcerting.'

Alice ran a grey tongue over her thin, painted lips. Felicity looked at her closely. The weekend at The Copse House Hotel came flooding back to her. She had paid good money for those lips to have vats of collagen pumped into them and just look at them now, she thought. Thin as blades of grass.

'Lydia?' she gasped.

'Oh, fuck, it's you,' replied Alice, mildly out of character. Her agent would surely have words with her about such a slippage.

'What on earth are you doing here?' cried Felicity and Geoffrey in unison. Seeing Lydia dressed like this was fantastic. Felicity bristled with delight. Geoffrey, on the other hand, turned a whiter shade of pale and wheezed uncontrollably.

'Thought I'd try something different,' Lydia explained, wiggling ominously. 'Actually, Jasper got me onto it. He's one of the Queen's Soldiers. He's going to do some chopping later on.

'So, will they have The Queen of Hearts?'

'Of course! We couldn't leave her out, could we?'

'I'm so relieved. I always say that it's so much better when plays keep to the original storyline, don't you agree?'

'Absolutely. Anyway, better get on,' said Lydia, finally pulling her bare backside away from Geoffrey's nose. 'I'm coming back on in a minute as the Cheshire Cat and it's quite a big costume change.'

'I quite understand. I'll tell James that I saw you.'

Lydia swivelled round and tweaked Geoffrey's right cheek. 'Love ya!' she shrilled and disappeared into the wings.

Felicity turned to Roger. 'That was a pleasant surprise. Alice used to live with my boyfriend, James,' she explained. 'I think I need another drink.'

Geoffrey collapsed back into his chair, relieved that he could still breathe properly. It had been quite a close call, after all. Roger looked at his old chum sitting open-mouthed. 'Everything all right, Geoffrey?' he asked.

'Not quite.' Geoffrey pulled himself upright. 'Yesterday, I made a rather rash proposal of marriage.' Roger politely raised his eyebrows. 'Alice is to be the next Mrs Carter.' Geoffrey could feel his shrivelled heart thrashing around precariously beneath his tired ribs as the plans for his forthcoming nuptials were revealed. 'The wedding has been set for a month hence.'

'I see,' replied Roger. 'That explains a lot.'

Felicity, meanwhile, was star-struck, enraptured by the surreal performance of the nimble pensioners. She clapped her hands wildly as the motley crew whirled and twirled right in front of her eyes with moves that could only have been invented by an Olympic gymnast.

Finally, The Queen of Hearts made her spectacular entrance. Geoffrey and Roger (the former having made a speedy recovery after absorbing his fiancee's revelations, and, in particular, joyfully observing that her flexible joints could add literally hours of thrill and variety to their marital bed) were once again beside themselves in awe of the elderly lady who twirled with the greatest of ease around and around her pole. They rose from their seats and cheered vigorously as she threw one leg and then another into the air displaying her nether regions without a modicum of modesty.

'This is so much better than the Christmas production at Lincoln's Inn, don't you agree?' said Roger.

'Without doubt.' Geoffrey sipped some much needed vino blanco. He turned to whisper in Roger's ear. 'I don't know how they stay so supple, do you?'

'No idea. Possibly it's the HRT.'

Felicity watched, dumb-struck, as the Queen of Hearts completed her act by hurling jam tarts out of an orifice that had surely not been made by God for that purpose and she could only hope that He was not privy to this display. Such an achievement could surely have only been accomplished by a lot of practice and an unusually developed muscular system, Felicity surmised, and had it not been for that last demonstration her whole outlook on lap dancing might have been altered positively forever.

Finally, after mounds of homemade pastry had been "flung" over the crazed audience's heads, the stunning performance ground to a halt. Felicity, assuming correctly that she could not possibly have been left unscathed after such a remarkable display, touched the top of her head and felt a lump of sticky jam rapidly drying, entwining itself in the fur of her velveteen ears. Rats, she thought, I'll have to pay for the outfit to be dry-cleaned. She glared harshly at The Queen, hoping to convey her displeasure.

Somewhat surprisingly, her glare was returned. The Queen, not used to anything but a full house appreciation of her accomplished Tart Propulsion Act marched directly over to Felicity's table, ready for a right royal confrontation. However, when she was only a few feet away, she stopped suddenly in her tracks and turned quickly, fleeing her adoring audience and squashing strawberry jam into the polished wooden stage with her Queenly shoes.

'I wonder what was wrong with her?' asked Roger, very aware that his employee had shown some displeasure to Her Highness. Felicity took a deep breath before replying.

'That, Roger, was James' mother.'

'I see.'

'And I can't say that I had previously been made aware of her talents.'

'Well,' said Roger, swigging back the remains of his glass of wine. 'That explains a lot, too.'

THE SUPER BITCH

Later that night, a light breeze blew around the building site outside Sarah's home. Slowly it lifted torn pieces of paper high into the sky, up over Clapham Common and towards Battersea Park. As the wind dropped, the paper floated down and settled, as rubbish, in the gutters of South London. A young man in need of rest in the early hours of the following morning sat on the kerbside and picked up one of the ripped pieces of paper. It was part of a crumpled photograph of a young, smiling woman embracing two beautiful children.

Months ago, Mr Connolly had given the photograph, taken on one of the happiest days Mrs Connolly had ever known, to Felicity in preparation for trial. After taking the file from Felicity's room, Sarah had torn what she could into shreds and then hurled the remains into the dump. Luckily, the cherished photograph had escaped.

So, who was the real Super Bitch Lawyer?

THE END

Synopsis

'How to be a Super Bitch Lawyer' is a dark, farcical tale story concerning lawyers at the antiquated firm of Meade Pullen and Co in the 1990s. They are all secretly yearning for promotion to partnership level but each has a very different idea as to how this may be achieved.

Felicity Garrett attempts to follow the obvious route to partnership by working hard and making a great deal of money for the firm regardless of whom she tramples upon in her quest; meek and lovely Sarah has to spend many a night out with the firm's clients, thus leaving her boyfriend free to embark on an affair with her beautiful sister; and John will do anything to gain partnership to avoid the wrath of his testosterone-fuelled wife.

Meanwhile, Roger, the senior partner, aware that the firm is in a chaotic financial position, has to forge a secret deal with the firm's benefactor to keep the firm afloat. Also amidst this dilemma, Roger has to deal with a tight-fisted managing partner, an obscure employment department and a six-fingered practice manager.

And who is the real Super Bitch?

Autobiographical note

Anna Corsellis grew up in Cardiff and attended Howell's school, Llandaf. She spent periods of time during her childhood living in Boston, Massachusetts and in New Cavendish Street, London. She qualified as a solicitor in 1992 and became a partner and Head of the firm's Clinical Negligence Department in 1996. She is currently a lecturer on the Legal Practice Course in Holborn. Anna lives in Chiswick with her husband, a criminal barrister, and three children. *How To Be a Super Bitch Lawyer* is her first novel.

Printed in the USA
CPSIA information can be obtained
at www.ICGtesting.com
LVHW042309160924
791282LV00004B/29